New Year's Scone and the Missing Snowglobe (with recipes in the back)

A winter cozy mystery with an amateur sleuth and culinary clues

The Cozy Nook Bakery Mysteries

Book 1

Juniper Lane

Contents

Chapter 1

Snow sifted down over Frostberry Hollow like powdered sugar over a cooling cake.

Mara Linden stood in the middle of her bakery and watched it through the big front window, her breath fogging the glass. The town's main street lay almost empty, still half-asleep on the first Saturday of the new year. Only the warm yellow glow of the streetlamps and the faint outline of the church steeple showed through the gentle curtain of snow.

Behind her, Cozy Nook Bakery and Gifts hummed with softer light. The ovens whispered and clicked. The scent of cinnamon and butter soaked into the old wooden beams. A pot of coffee murmured on the back counter, the sound steady and comforting.

This was her world now.

Mara hugged her cardigan tighter over her flour-dusted T-shirt and turned away from the window. She had come in before five, too restless to lie in bed and stare at the ceiling of the apartment above the shop. The thought of a brand new year in a brand new town had set her nerves flickering, and sleep had been impossible. So she did the one thing that always steadied her.

She baked.

A row of baking trays waited on the long prep table, each lined with lavender parchment. Blackberry scone dough rested in plump triangles, speckled with dark berries and orange zest. Beside them, a pan of cinnamon rolls rose slowly, their spirals just visible beneath a cloth.

Mara reached for the nearest tray and brushed a light coat of cream across the top of each scone. Her movements were quick but careful. Ten years of managing people in a corporate office had left her with restless hands and a constant hum of stress behind her eyes. Months here in Frostberry Hollow had not erased that hum, but the rhythm of measuring and shaping and glazing had dulled its sharpest edges.

"Today is going to be fine," she murmured to the dough. "You will behave. You will rise. You will not crumble at the wrong moment, and neither will I."

The oven timer beeped. She slid the first tray inside and closed the door, heat blooming against her face. The glass fogged over, then cleared to show the pale shapes inside.

New Year's weekend. The charity brunch. Her first big social test as the new owner of Cozy Nook.

Mara inhaled deeply and let the warm, sweet air fill her lungs. Everything smelled of cinnamon, vanilla, and a faint hint of citrus. If the town decided to turn against her, at least the bakery would smell kind while it happened.

She laughed at herself and shook off the thought. Not helpful.

On the far side of the room, past the display counter and the chalkboard menu, a glass cabinet stood under its own pool of light. Snowglobes of every size and style rested inside, their glass domes catching and bending the glow. Miniature cabins, twinkling streetlamps, ice skaters on tiny frozen ponds, snow-covered bookshops. A whole village of captured winters.

Mara crossed to the cabinet, wiped an invisible speck of dust from the glass, and unlocked the door. The click sounded loud in the quiet.

"Morning, little worlds," she said under her breath.

Her aunt Iris had said that for years. When Mara inherited the place after Iris's sudden stroke, the words came with the keys and the lease and the half written recipes. They felt like part of the job.

Mara lifted one of the globes with both hands. It was slightly larger than the others, the glass cool against her palms. Inside, a miniature bridge arched over a frozen creek. Tiny evergreens lined the banks, each tipped with snow. On the bridge stood a single streetlamp, its post delicately painted black, the suggestion of a glow at the top.

She tipped the globe gently and watched the snow drift and swirl.

This was the prototype for her New Beginnings design. The final version for the charity auction sat in her small workroom upstairs, waiting for a last touch of paint. Winning bidders at the brunch would compete for a handful of donated items from local businesses, and this globe was her contribution.

"I hope people like you," Mara whispered. "I really need them to like you."

The bell over the door gave a soft jingle.

She nearly dropped the globe.

"Good grief," she muttered, steadying herself as she slid the globe back into place. "We are not starting the year by smashing anything."

She locked the cabinet before turning, wiping her hands quickly on her apron.

"Morning," she called.

"Morning, dear."

Ellie Marsh stood just inside the door, stamping snow from her boots. She wore a crimson wool coat, buttoned to her chin, and a knitted hat with an enormous pom-pom that trembled when she moved. Her cheeks glowed pink from the cold.

"You are early," Mara said. "We do not open for another thirty minutes."

Ellie sniffed the air and closed her eyes for a moment.

"You smell open," she said. "And besides, I brought bribes."

She lifted the canvas tote bag on her arm and let it swing. Papers rustled inside.

Mara smiled despite herself. "All right. For bribes, we make exceptions."

She moved behind the counter and reached for a mug. "Coffee?"

"If you are offering, the answer is always yes." Ellie unwound her scarf and set it on the back of a chair, then crossed to the glass cabinet. "I wanted to see how my little neighbors are doing."

"Your neighbors?" Mara poured the coffee and slid it across the counter.

"Of course." Ellie leaned close to the glass with a fond expression. "We are practically roommates. I see them every day."

"They are not finished yet," Mara said. "Well, some of them are. Some are still prototypes. I keep changing my mind about the details."

"That is half the charm." Ellie accepted the mug and wrapped both hands around it with a contented sigh. "Besides, you should hear yourself. Do you realize you say we when you talk about the shop now?"

Mara froze.

"I do not."

"You do." Ellie took a careful sip and nodded, satisfied. "It used to be Aunt Iris's shop, Aunt Iris's baking, Aunt Iris's crazy snowglobes. Now it is our oven, our morning rush, our little worlds. That is progress."

Warmth that had nothing to do with the coffee moved through Mara's chest. She tried not to show it too obviously.

"I am trying to respect what she built," she said. "I still feel like I am borrowing someone else's life."

Ellie's gaze softened.

"You are not borrowing," she said. "You are continuing. She would be proud to see the ovens still working and the globes still shining. She would be tickled to see how many people are talking about your scones."

"Talking good things, I hope."

"Mostly." Ellie set her tote bag on a table and pulled out a stack of flyers. "Which brings me to the bribe. I promised the charity committee we would post these by the register."

Mara wiped her hands again and took one of the flyers.

Frostberry Hollow New Year Brunch, the heading read, in looping blue letters. A list of sponsors and donors ran underneath. The Cozy Nook Bakery and Gifts had a spot in the middle, in small but real type.

Her throat tightened.

"They spelled it correctly," she said. "That is already better than my last job."

"Companies have a talent for misspelling their employees' names," Ellie said. "Towns, on the other hand, tend to get the local businesses right. Especially when those businesses feed them."

She tapped the line that mentioned Mara's contribution. One handcrafted winter snowglobe and a selection of seasonal baked goods.

"Nervous?" Ellie asked.

Mara spread the flyers like a fan on the counter and reached for tape.

"A little," she said. "I have done events before. Holiday luncheons and corporate mixers. Our office did a team building retreat with a chocolate fountain that nearly burned the building down. The stakes feel different here."

"Of course they do. In a company you are just trying to survive the fiscal year. Here you are trying to belong." Ellie smiled. "Different game."

Mara taped one flyer to the side of the pastry case, another near the register.

"What if they do not like the gluten free scones?" she asked.

"They will like them." Ellie's tone left no room for argument. "I tested three versions and this one is perfect."

"You are not exactly unbiased. You like anything with sugar."

"Not true. I have standards." Ellie sniffed. "Some sugar is far better than others."

They shared a laugh. The tension behind Mara's eyes eased, just a little.

Outside, a car door slammed. The sound carried faintly through the glass.

"Your first customer of the year," Ellie said. "Smile in a welcoming manner. I will sit over here and practice looking like a wise village elder."

"You are not old," Mara said.

"Tell my knees that."

The bell chimed again. A gust of cold air slipped in, along with the scent of exhaust and snow.

"Morning," Mara called, straightening.

Mr. Kline shuffled through the door, bundled in a bulky coat and wool cap that had seen better winters. He smelled faintly of tobacco and motor oil. A retired mechanic, he had adopted the Cozy Nook as his unofficial office. He lived for hot coffee and gossip.

"Happy new year," he said, stomping his boots on the mat. "Thought I would beat the rush."

"You usually do," Mara said, reaching for another mug. "The usual?"

"Unless you invented something new overnight." He peered at the chalkboard. "What is a frosted cranberry scone cake? And why does it sound like it wants to jump into my mouth?"

Ellie chuckled softly from her corner table.

"It is a shared dessert," Mara said. "You can take a wedge with your coffee or buy a whole one for later. Very moist, not too sweet. Some lemon in the glaze. I am still testing the name."

"You are testing it on me." Mr. Kline rubbed his hands together. "In that case, I volunteer as tribute."

"Coffee and a slice," Mara said. "Coming right up."

She plated a generous piece and set it on the counter along with the steaming mug. Mr. Kline took a bite and closed his eyes.

"Huh," he said after a moment. "This is... very bad. You should probably give the rest to me so no one else suffers."

Mara laughed. "That is not original, you know. Every man who has ever liked a dessert says that."

"I am a traditionalist." He took another bite. "You taking all this to the brunch?"

"Some of it," she said. "Mostly the blackberry scones and a cinnamon roll tray. And the snowglobe."

His eyes slid toward the cabinet.

"The one you showed the committee?" he asked. "The bridge and the lamp?"

"That is the one."

Mr. Kline nodded slowly. "Got a nice feel to it. Like a little promise in glass."

"A promise of what?"

"That you can walk from one year to the next without falling into the creek." He shrugged. "People like that idea. Especially around here. Not every year has been kind."

Mara thought of the stacks of unpaid bills she had found in Iris's desk, the half finished recipe cards, the notebook full of ideas Iris never had time to try. Her aunt had always been in motion, bouncing between ovens and glass and customers with fierce energy. After the stroke, it had all gone still.

"I hope this year is kinder," she said quietly.

"It will be." Ellie's voice came from behind her. "We will make it so, one scone at a time."

The bell chimed again, and the next half hour dissolved into movement. A trio of teenagers stopped in for hot chocolate before heading to the frozen pond. A nurse from the small clinic down the road grabbed a pastry on her way to an early shift. A delivery driver stamped snow from his boots and ordered a cinnamon roll to go.

By the time Mara hung the Open sign in the window, the bakery already hummed with life. Mugs clinked. Chairs scraped. Conversations overlapped in a cozy rumble.

The town was waking up.

Mara worked the register, filled plates, smiled until her cheeks ached. The knot of worry in her stomach eased each time someone said they would see her at the brunch, that they were looking forward to her baked goods, that the town was lucky to have her.

This, she thought, was the good part. The part that made the anxiety worth it.

She did not think about the long hours or the thin bank account. She did not think about the corporate life she had left behind, with its meetings and performance reviews and endless fluorescent lights. Here, at least, exhaustion came with the smell of cinnamon and the sound of laughter.

She had just finished wiping a stray smear of icing from the edge of the pastry case when the door chimed once more. A curl of wind swirled in and scattered a few sugar crystals on the floor.

"Okay," she said without turning. "Whoever you are, you are required to compliment something you smell before I let you sit down."

"That seems unfair to those of us who cannot smell much before coffee."

The familiar voice brought a grin to her face. She looked up to see Jenna Price shoulder the door closed with a hip, her camera bag thumping against her side.

"You are late," Mara said.

"It is eight-ten. That is not late."

"In a bakery, that is nearly lunchtime." Mara nodded at the clock. "For the cinnamon rolls, anyway."

Jenna tossed her curls, sending a dusting of snowflakes onto the mat, and unwrapped her scarf.

"Excuse me for wanting to look presentable for the first weekend of the year," she said. "You never know who will walk in. Your future husband, a famous food blogger, the mayor of a small country who got lost in the snow."

"You have been watching too many holiday movies again."

"Occupational hazard." Jenna slung her bag onto a chair and leaned against the counter. "What is new? Any disasters yet?"

"Only if you count teenagers ordering triple marshmallows as a disaster," Mara said. "Otherwise, the morning has been surprisingly normal."

Ellie lifted a hand from her table. "We have had deep philosophical discussions about scones and the meaning of snowglobes."

"Ah, a regular Saturday, then." Jenna loosened her ponytail and grabbed an apron from the hook. "Tell me we still have at least one cinnamon roll. I need fuel before I start pointing my camera in people's faces."

"You need fuel before you start functioning as a human," Mara said. "Yes, there are cinnamon rolls. I made extra."

"Excellent." Jenna rounded the counter and peered into the baking trays. "You know the brunch committee is counting on you, right? Half the reason people buy tickets is for your pastries."

"That is a horrifying amount of pressure."

"Welcome to small town expectations." Jenna gave her a playful nudge. "Did you finish the snowglobe?"

"Mostly," Mara said. "The bridge and the lamp are done. I just need to paint the tiniest bit of light at the top. If my hand shakes, it will look like the lamp exploded instead of glowing, and then it becomes a very different kind of story."

"Exploding snowglobe of doom," Jenna said. "That sounds like a different genre entirely."

"This town is not ready for that genre," Ellie said dryly. "We prefer the one where nothing terrible ever happens for very long."

"You mean denial," Mr. Kline called from his table. "We are very good at that one."

The little circle of laughter that followed warmed Mara more than the hot ovens.

"See?" Jenna said. "They love you. You will be fine today."

Mara wished she shared Jenna's certainty.

"Maybe," she said. "It is just... the brunch feels important. Like a test I did not study for."

"You have been baking and crafting and stressing for three weeks," Jenna said. "If that is not studying, I do not know what is."

She lifted the camera from her bag and flipped the strap around her neck.

"Speaking of stress," Jenna said. "Harriet asked if I could grab a few early photos for the event page. She wants proof that everyone is excited and supportive and all that. So I may poke my lens into your workspace for a few shots. Show the magic behind the muffins."

"As long as you do not photograph the dirty mixing bowls in the sink," Mara said. "My magic has limits."

"Got it. Artistic angles only." Jenna snapped a quick photo of the bakery interior. "Look at this. The light on those snowglobes is perfect. That display case was meant for the homepage of a website."

"Let us keep them in the shop for now," Mara said. "The website can wait until I figure out the cash flow."

Jenna opened her mouth to answer, then glanced at the clock.

"Okay, focus," she said. "We have, what, three hours until you need to deliver the goods to the pavilion? Plenty of time. I will take photos and help you box everything. Ellie will keep the customers happy and the coffee flowing. You, my dear, will breathe."

She exaggerated a slow inhale and exhale. Mara rolled her eyes, but took the breath anyway.

The air that filled her lungs was warm, scented with sugar and spice and coffee and the faint metallic tang of snow carried in on coats and scarves. It did help.

"Fine," she said. "I will breathe. But only because you insisted."

"Good." Jenna raised the camera again. "Now pick up a scone and pretend you are about to change your life with it."

"That is a lot to ask of a pastry."

"You have not tasted your own baking lately, then."

Mara shook her head and reached for the tray of blackberry scones. The first batch had cooled on the rack, their tops golden, the berries just visible beneath the crust.

She held one up, and Jenna clicked the shutter. The camera beeped, capturing the moment.

"Perfect," Jenna said, checking the screen. "That is your new year right there. A woman, a scone, and a chance to start over."

Mara looked at the picture. The woman in it had flour on her cheek and a cautious smile. Her eyes held a mix of hope and worry that made Mara's chest tighten. She almost did not recognize herself.

"Send me that later," she said softly.

"Of course." Jenna slung the camera at her hip again. "We can use it when you, you know, become famous for your snowglobe mysteries and bakery delights."

"Let us survive today first."

"We will," Jenna said. "Trust me. What is the worst that could happen at a charity brunch?"

Ellie made a soft sound at her table, something between a laugh and a wince.

"Do not say that," she said. "You never tempt fate in Frostberry Hollow. The town has a long memory and a wicked sense of humor."

Mara smiled, but a strange little shiver worked its way down her spine, out of harmony with the cozy warmth of the room.

It was nothing, she told herself. Just nerves.

She turned back to the ovens, to the trays, to the familiar rhythm of baking. Outside the window, the snow continued to fall, quiet and steady, as if the world were holding its breath for whatever the new year would bring.

Chapter 2

The morning rush peaked just after nine, then settled into a comfortable lull. Chairs scraped softly as a few lingering customers chatted over warm drinks, and a steady hiss from the espresso machine filled the background like a familiar sigh. Snow still drifted outside, gentler now, as if the storm had grown tired.

Mara wiped the counter, humming under her breath. The gentle rhythm of cleaning helped keep her nerves steady. When she finished, she reached for a fresh tray of scones and set them behind the glass display. The bakery felt safe again, warm and bright, untouched by the anxieties of the coming event.

She had just started to refill the napkin holders when the bell above the door chimed.

The sound carried differently this time. Sharper. More pointed.

Mara straightened at once.

Owen Barrow stepped inside.

A cold gust followed him, carrying the brittle metallic scent of winter air. He closed the door with a gloved hand and brushed a few snowflakes from his shoulders. They melted almost instantly against the dark wool of his coat. His hair, peppered with gray at the temples, lay neatly in place, and his posture suggested someone who expected the world to arrange itself for his convenience.

Mara had seen him only a handful of times since moving to Frostberry Hollow, but each meeting had left her with the faint impression of standing too close to an unsheathed knife.

Today was no different.

His gaze swept over the bakery in a single, cool arc. It landed on the display case of pastries only briefly before shifting toward the snowglobe cabinet.

He stepped closer.

Mara felt her pulse nudge upward.

"Good morning, Mr. Barrow," she said, keeping her voice brisk but friendly. "Cold out there today."

He did not look at her yet. He stood with his hands clasped behind his back, studying the snowglobes with sudden and complete focus, as if each glass dome held a political secret.

"Cold," he repeated, still watching the display. "Yes. Winter does that."

Mara waited a moment, unsure if she was expected to respond. Owen's tone had the measured indifference of a man who enjoyed leaving others slightly off balance.

"Is there something I can help you find?" she asked.

He finally turned his head. His eyes were pale, the precise color of icy water beneath thin sunlight. They held no warmth.

"I saw your name on the brunch flyer," he said. "Quite a prominent donation. A snowglobe, is it? Handcrafted."

"Yes," Mara replied. "For the charity auction. It is a limited winter design."

Owen's gaze flicked to the cabinet again, then back to her. There was a faint tightening around his mouth, too controlled to be a smile.

"I suppose that is charming enough for our little town," he said. "Though I hope the quality lives up to the hype."

"It will," Mara said, her voice steady. "I take a lot of care with the details."

"So I see."

He reached out and tapped the glass with one knuckle. The action made Mara flinch even though the cabinet did not move. His focus settled on the New Beginnings prototype near the center shelf.

"What is this one called?" he asked.

"That is the prototype for the design going to the brunch," she said. "The final version has a few differences, but the bridge and lamp are the same. It represents a fresh start."

Owen's head tilted slightly, as if the concept amused him. He leaned in closer, studying the tiny figure of the lamp on the snow covered bridge.

"A fresh start," he echoed. "People in this town cling to that idea like it is a raft in a storm."

Mara felt the comment rustle through the air like a chill draft.

"I think people appreciate symbols of hope," she said.

"They appreciate symbols of anything," he replied. "Hope. Anger. Nostalgia. If you package it neatly enough, they will buy it."

He stepped back from the glass.

"Well," he said. "At least you understand your customers."

His eyes drifted toward the pastry counter. She saw the moment he spotted the sign for gluten free blackberry scones.

"A gluten free option," he said. "Bold choice. Not something this town usually bothers with."

"It is part of the brunch menu," Mara said. "And a few regulars appreciate it. I tested several versions to get the texture right."

"Texture," Owen repeated with a faintly unimpressed tone. "I imagine it tastes like chalk."

"It does not," she said before she could stop herself. "I promise the recipe is solid."

"Prove it."

Mara blinked at him.

"Prove it?" she repeated.

"Yes," he said. "Give me one."

His voice carried no hint of friendliness. It did not sound like a man eager for a sample. It sounded like a challenge.

Mara lifted her chin. She placed a scone on a small plate and set it on the counter in front of him. Owen did not pick it up right away. Instead he stood very still, studying her, studying the bakery, studying everything like he needed to take apart the room and reassemble it to fit his liking.

Finally he reached for the scone.

He took a deliberate bite.

He chewed slowly, without expression. A faint smudge of blackberry stained the corner of his mouth. He did not wipe it away.

Mara waited, resisting the urge to fidget.

After several long seconds, he swallowed and set the half eaten scone back on the plate.

"I have had worse," he said.

It was neither compliment nor insult. It was a dismissal. A judgment that kept her firmly at arm's length.

"I am glad to hear it," Mara said evenly.

Owen clasped his hands behind his back again.

"This town has very little competition among bakeries," he said. "People are easily impressed. Remember that when the brunch starts. It is not difficult to stand out here."

Mara felt irritation push at the edges of her patience. She forced herself to breathe.

"I am doing my best," she said. "I want to be part of the community."

"Good," he said lightly. "Then you should learn how the community actually works."

He leaned closer, voice dropping so only she could hear.

"Property defines everything in Frostberry Hollow. Who owns it. Who wants it. Who is foolish enough to sell it to the wrong person."

She felt her stomach tighten.

"I do not follow," she said.

"You will," Owen replied. "Sooner or later, you will."

He took another glance around the bakery.

"This shop has potential," he said. "A bit run down in some corners, but it could shine with the right guidance. Perhaps we should talk about the building sometime. And the property line behind it."

Mara stiffened.

"I have no interest in selling," she said.

His expression remained perfectly neutral.

"You never know what the year may bring."

He slipped on his gloves and moved toward the door. Before pushing it open, he paused and glanced back at the snowglobe cabinet one last time.

"It is an interesting piece," he said. "That bridge and lamp. I suppose some people find comfort in small illusions."

"There is nothing illusory about craftsmanship," Mara said quietly.

Owen studied her for a moment. Something unreadable flickered behind his eyes, a thin glint, like a fish surfacing beneath a frozen pond.

Then he nodded once.

"Enjoy your morning."

He left without waiting for a reply.

The bell chimed faintly, the cold air slipping in behind him.

Mara let out the breath she had been holding.

* * *

The door closed with a soft but final click, and the rumble of Owen's car engine faded into the snowy quiet outside. Mara stood still for a moment, letting the tension drain slowly from her shoulders.

Behind her, Ellie let out a breath that sounded like she had been holding it through the entire conversation.

"Well," Ellie said, adjusting her hat. "He has lost none of his charm."

Mara turned to her. "Is he always like that?"

"Always," Ellie said. "He treats people the same way he treats real estate. Everything is a negotiation. Everyone is a potential acquisition."

Jenna stepped out from the back hallway holding a tray of freshly iced cookies. She froze halfway to the counter.

"Please tell me the temperature in here just dropped because you opened the door," Jenna said. "Because it feels like someone dragged a giant block of ice through the building."

"That was Owen Barrow," Mara said.

Jenna set the tray down. "Oh. That explains it."

"He tasted the gluten free scone," Mara said. "Then told me he has had worse."

"Which means it was delicious," Jenna said. "He does not compliment anything unless it raises his stock value."

"He also hinted about buying the building. And said something about the property line."

Ellie folded her hands over her mug. "That would be like him. He has been trying to expand his holdings for years. He likes control. Some say he needs it."

"I do not plan on selling," Mara said firmly.

"No one expects you to," Ellie said. "Though Owen tends to push harder when told no."

"That is comforting," Mara muttered.

Jenna leaned closer. "Did he say anything else? He has this way of talking that makes you feel like he knows something you do not."

"He talked about the snowglobe," Mara said. "The prototype. He studied it like he was looking for a secret."

Ellie raised her brows. "Really? He showed that much interest in a snowglobe?"

"He asked what it symbolized," Mara said. "And then he made a comment about people buying illusions."

"That sounds exactly like him," Jenna said. "He thinks sentiment is a weakness. He once told me that hope is for people without business sense."

Mara blinked. "He said that to you?"

"Yes. I was seventeen at the time and taking photos for the Fall Harvest Festival. I think he considered it a valuable life lesson."

Ellie snorted softly. "He should consider teaching manners."

Mara wiped her hands on a towel, trying to shake off the last threads of discomfort.

"Do you think he came in just to cause trouble?" Mara asked.

"No," Ellie said thoughtfully. "He came in because he wanted something."

"Which is worse," Jenna added.

Mara frowned. "What could he want from me? I barely know him."

"Maybe he just wanted to rattle you," Jenna said. "Some people enjoy that kind of power."

Ellie sipped her coffee again. "Owen has been involved in three property disputes in the last two years. Each time, he pushed until the other side folded. If he thinks you are vulnerable, he might assume you will fold too."

Mara felt a cold knot forming deep in her stomach.

"I am not looking for a fight," she said quietly.

"No one said you were," Ellie replied. "But living in this town means you will cross paths with people who carry old grudges and private ambitions. Owen carries more than most."

A sudden lull settled between them. The bakery's warm light felt slightly dimmer.

Jenna broke the silence by straightening the tray of cookies.

"Okay," she said. "We are not letting Owen's frostbite personality ruin your morning. You have baking to finish, a charity brunch to prepare for, and a town full of people who actually enjoy your presence. So we will ignore him for now."

Mara managed a smile. "Easier said than done."

"We will make it easier," Jenna insisted. "Starting with music."

She grabbed her phone, scrolled through a playlist, and set upbeat acoustic guitar music playing through the small speaker on the counter. The warm melody wrapped itself around the room, soft and steady.

Ellie nodded approvingly. "Much better."

Mara leaned on the counter for a moment, letting the warmth return to her bones. "Thank you," she said.

"Always," Jenna said.

They eased back into their tasks, though Mara's thoughts drifted repeatedly to the snowglobe cabinet. She kept catching herself glancing in that direction, imagining Owen's pale gaze lingering there. It felt strange, as if his interest had been less curiosity and more calculation.

But she brushed the thought aside. There was too much to do, and the brunch would not wait for her nerves to calm.

The day continued in a gentle rhythm. Customers came and went, drifting in with the cold and leaving with warm pastry boxes tucked under their arms. Mara made coffee, organized orders, refilled sugar jars, and chatted with regulars who had known her aunt for years.

The hours passed faster than she expected.

By late afternoon, the bakery had quieted again. The last customer left with a cheerful wave, and the bell fell silent. Outside, the streetlights flickered on, painting long streaks of gold across the soft snow.

Jenna hung her apron on its hook.

"I have to head out," she said. "Harriet wants me to check the pavilion decorations before the evening frost hits everything. I will swing by again tomorrow morning."

"Thank you for today," Mara said. "Have fun dealing with Harriet."

"I will try," Jenna said. "If I disappear, assume the tinsel monster got me."

Ellie snickered softly. "Stay vigilant."

Jenna grinned, then slipped out into the cold evening.

Ellie gathered her coat and hat as well, moving slowly, as if reluctant to leave the warm shelter of the bakery.

"Before I go," Ellie said, "remember something."

"What is that?" Mara asked.

"Owen Barrow does not define this day. Or this bakery. Or you."

Mara felt her chest tighten again, but this time with something warmer.

"Thank you," she said softly.

Ellie reached out and squeezed her hand.

"You are doing fine," she said. "Better than fine. Iris chose well."

Then she tucked her scarf around her neck and stepped out into the soft snowfall.

The bakery felt very quiet after both women left.

Mara turned off the overhead lights one by one, leaving only the cabinet glow and the warm lamp on the counter. She wiped the tables again, though they were already clean. She cleaned the coffee machine, organized the counters, and straightened the display trays.

When everything was in order, she walked to the snowglobe cabinet.

She unlocked it with the small silver key and lifted the New Beginnings prototype.

The glass felt cold against her palms.

She tilted it gently, watching the snow swirl inside, catching the tiny bridge and frozen creek in a drifting white storm.

The little lamp at the center flickered faintly with painted light.

A symbol of hope.

A fresh start.

Yet Owen Barrow had looked at it like a puzzle waiting to be solved. Or a secret waiting to be uncovered.

Mara set the globe back in its place and locked the cabinet again.

Something told her Owen had not come in simply to taste a scone. He had been interested in something else. The building. The property. The snowglobe. Something.

She turned the last light switch near the door.

The bakery fell into quiet twilight, warmed by the glow of the cabinet.

Mara stood for a moment, listening to the soft hum of the refrigerators and the faint sound of wind against the windows.

Whatever Owen Barrow wanted, she sensed he was not finished with her yet.

Tomorrow would bring the brunch.

And something in her bones whispered that it would bring more than that.

She locked the door behind her, pulled her coat tight, and stepped into the snowy evening, unaware that this day had been her last peaceful one for a long time.

Chapter 3

The next morning dawned in shades of pearl and pale gold, the kind of winter light that made everything feel softer and quieter than it truly was. Frostberry Hollow stirred slowly. Smoke curled from chimneys. Footprints pressed into fresh snow along the sidewalks. A faint mist clung to the evergreen branches like a secret.

Inside the Cozy Nook Bakery, the world could not have been more different.

The ovens glowed hot. Pans clanged. The mixer hummed in steady circles. Warm scents drifted through the air in layers, each unfolding into the next: butter, citrus zest, caramelizing sugar, dark berries, and a hint of vanilla.

Mara wiped her hands on her apron for the fifth time in ten minutes.

"I will never get through this list if I keep fussing," she muttered. "Focus."

The bakery counters had been transformed into organized chaos. Rows of measuring cups, bowls of sifted flour, racks lined with cooling parchment, trays waiting for their turn in the oven. The charity brunch order sat at the forefront of everything. Two dozen cinnamon rolls. Three dozen blackberry scones. Two trays of cranberry scone cake slices. A set of gluten free pastries in their own corner, guarded like precious artifacts.

Mara pulled a tray of scones from the oven and breathed in the scent as steam curled upward.

Perfect.

Golden tops. Crispy edges. A soft center she had tested enough times to memorize.

She set the tray on a cooling rack and immediately began brushing the tops with a warm maple glaze. As she worked, she found herself humming without realizing it. Not a tune with a name. Just something soft and steady that kept her hands moving with calm purpose.

Behind her, the door to the upstairs workroom stood half open. Light glowed from inside, illuminating the edge of her paint table where the partially finished snowglobe rested. She would have to finish it before the day was over.

For now, though, the pastries demanded her full attention.

She finished glazing the tray and slid another batch into the oven. As she closed the door, the bell above the bakery entrance chimed faintly.

"That better be Jenna with more coffee," she said under her breath.

Instead it was Ellie.

The older woman stepped inside with her usual flair, wrapped in a checked wool coat and a scarf that looked hand knitted by someone who believed color was a battle they intended to win. She carried a cloth grocery bag over one arm and a small plastic tub in her free hand.

"I brought reinforcements," Ellie announced.

"You brought… berries?" Mara guessed, eyeing the tub.

"Better," Ellie said. "Sweet cream. Some of the brunch guests like to dollop it on their pastries. Harriet insisted we make some available. Apparently tradition is more important than the baker's sanity."

Mara set the tub on the counter. "I will find a way to keep it chilled."

Ellie surveyed the bakery with approval.

"Look at all this," she said. "You have turned this place into a pastry command center."

"That is one word for it," Mara said.

"Then the correct word is impressive," Ellie replied. "Iris would be glowing."

Mara felt warmth move through her chest at the mention of her aunt. Not the sharp ache of grief. Something gentler. Something like pride.

"I just want everything to go well today," she said.

"And it will," Ellie said. "Though I did hear a few whispers in town this morning. People are curious after Owen's little visit yesterday."

Mara paused in the middle of reaching for a mixing bowl.

"That was fast," she said.

"This is Frostberry Hollow," Ellie replied. "Information here travels faster than snowmelt in spring."

"Were the whispers… concerning?" Mara asked.

"Well," Ellie said, lowering her voice, "people know Owen has been sniffing around properties again. Some wonder if he came here to stir trouble. Others wonder if he came looking for an advantage at the brunch. He likes to have leverage before public events."

"That is not reassuring."

"No," Ellie said cheerfully. "But it is true."

Mara sighed.

"Try not to worry," Ellie added. "The town gossips are always ten steps ahead of reality. Right now they are probably inventing a story about Owen planning to turn the pavilion into a high end spa."

Mara snorted. "He would probably try."

"Oh, absolutely," Ellie said. "He would name it something like Serenity Falls and charge a kidney for each membership."

Despite herself, Mara laughed.

She moved to the counter again and began scooping flour for the next batch. The sensation of the cool powder settling between her fingers steadied her. Baking had always helped her keep her center, even when nerves pressed in.

Ellie tied on an apron from the hook and rolled up her sleeves.

"What can I do?" she asked.

"Packaging," Mara said instantly. "If you can start folding the pastry boxes, I will fill them once the scones cool."

"Done," Ellie said.

She got to work on the folding station near the front window. The gentle creasing of cardboard filled the air in soft rhythmic clicks.

Ten minutes passed. Then fifteen. The bakery grew warm with the comforting noises of shared work.

Finally, Mara glanced toward the upstairs workroom.

"I should finish the snowglobe before we run out of time," she said. "Can you manage things down here?"

"Go," Ellie said without looking up. "I will keep the pastries safe. No one will sneak in and steal a cinnamon roll on my watch."

Mara set down her spatula and wiped her hands. She paused by the coffee pot, poured a half cup, and carried it up the narrow staircase.

The workroom felt quieter than the bakery below. The wooden floor creaked under her steps. Shelves lined the walls, filled with tiny jars of paint, rows of miniature trees, little bridges, and boxes of snowglobe bases. Sunlight filtered through the window, resting like a soft hand across the table surface.

At the center of the room sat her nearly finished piece.

The New Beginnings snowglobe.

She approached it carefully, as if it might bruise with too much enthusiasm.

The small bridge arched gracefully over the frozen creek. She had painted the wooden planks with a muted gray wash and added tiny streaks of snow at the edges. The lamp stood at the center of the bridge, tall and slender, topped with a glass bead that suggested a faint glow. She needed one more coat of pale yellow paint to make it shimmer in the right light.

Mara sat, took a steady breath, and began working.

With a brush the size of a toothpick, she touched the bead with a pinpoint of paint, letting the color adjust under her hand.

The world shrank to the size of the miniature.

Each detail mattered. The cracks in the bridge. The arrangement of the snow. The texture of the frozen water. She worked methodically, letting the calm sink into her bones. It felt peaceful. Meditative. She forgot the pastries, the gossip, and even Owen for a few minutes.

A soft knock at the bottom of the stairs startled her.

"Everything okay?" Jenna called up.

"In here," Mara said. "Come up."

Jenna appeared a moment later, camera slung over her shoulder, curls springing in every direction. She held a small paper bag in one hand.

"I brought muffins," she said. "From the market down the street."

"You brought food to the bakery?" Mara asked.

"These are not for customers," Jenna said. "These are for stressed bakers. Completely different category."

She set the bag on the corner of the desk and leaned over the snowglobe.

"Oh wow," she whispered. "It is even prettier than the prototype. Look at the way the bridge lines up. And the lamp. You nailed it."

"I am almost done," Mara said. "I just need to seal the paint once it dries."

Jenna raised her camera. "Mind if I get a few pictures?"

"Go ahead."

She snapped several shots, adjusting her angle, moving closer, pulling back.

"These will look great online," she said.

"Online?" Mara blinked.

"Yes. Harriet wants a preview post for the brunch page. Something to build hype. I figured your snowglobe should get the spotlight."

Mara felt her stomach flip.

"No pressure," Jenna added. "Just the entire town seeing this in advance."

"That is not comforting," Mara said.

"It was not meant to be," Jenna said, winking. "But trust me, they will love it."

She stepped back, lowering her camera.

"Ellie said the bakery looks gorgeous this morning," she said. "Do you want some photos downstairs too?"

"Yes," Mara said. "But wait until I finish this coat."

"I can do that."

Jenna wandered to the window and peered outside. Her expression shifted.

"That is weird," she murmured.

"What is?"

"I thought someone was standing across the street," Jenna said, "but there is nothing now. Probably just the mailman."

Mara joined her at the window.

The street below was empty. A single car sat parked near the corner, dusted with snow. A dog trotted past, nose buried in a drift. No person in sight.

"It might have been a reflection," Mara said.

"Maybe," Jenna said, though she sounded unconvinced.

Mara returned to the desk, heart beating a little faster.

People stared into shop windows all the time. Nothing strange about it.

Except today it felt strange.

And familiar.

A shadow. A stillness. A presence that had hovered at the edge of her awareness since yesterday.

She brushed the feeling aside and refocused on the snowglobe.

There was still work to do.

* * *

The paint dried with a soft sheen, just enough to brighten the tiny lamp without overwhelming the delicate scene around it. Mara exhaled slowly, steadier now.

"That is it," she said. "It is done."

Jenna leaned in again. "It is perfect. Really. People are going to fight over this at the auction. Politely, of course. With winter manners. Probably."

Mara smiled at that.

She carried the snowglobe downstairs, each step taken with deliberate care. She set it gently inside the glass cabinet to await final packing for the brunch.

Ellie turned from the folding table when she heard the soft click of the cabinet door.

"Look at that," she said, clutching a half folded pastry box in her hands. "It catches the light just right. If that does not charm people, nothing will."

"Let us hope charm is enough," Mara said.

"You worry too much," Ellie answered. "This town might gossip about everything from mail delivery delays to who wore what scarf, but they love a good handcrafted piece. They are proud of them. Always have been."

Jenna lifted her camera again and began capturing the scene. The soft glow from the cabinet lights reflected in the glass, creating a warm halo around the tiny bridge.

"This is beautiful," Jenna said. "Like a little world inside a lantern."

Mara felt a small flush of pride. "Thank you."

They returned to the bustle of preparation. Ellie folded more boxes, stacking them into a tower on the counter. Mara filled trays with cooled pastries, arranging each one with the kind of careful attention most people reserved for works of art. Jenna moved around the bakery in a flowing path, adjusting angles, shooting from behind the display case, crouching near the counter, stepping back to capture a wide shot of the warm, glowing interior.

"This is perfect," Jenna said as she reviewed her screen. "The lighting, the snow outside, the pastries. This could be on a magazine cover."

"I do not think magazines come looking for hidden bakeries in mountain towns," Mara said.

"Not yet," Jenna replied. "Give it time."

Mara was sealing a tray of cinnamon rolls when Ellie cleared her throat.

"So," Ellie said casually, "do either of you want to hear the newest round of market gossip?"

Jenna froze mid-step. "Always."

Mara glanced over. "If it is about Owen Barrow, I might not be ready for it."

"Oh it is about him," Ellie said. "And you should hear it."

Mara set down her cloth and leaned on the counter.

"Someone saw him arguing with Mark Whitcomb yesterday afternoon behind the Old Mill Market. Loudly. And honestly, Mark never raises his voice. He hardly raises his posture. But the witness said he looked ready to start a fight."

"About what?" Jenna asked.

"Property," Ellie said. "That is always his subject. Apparently Owen wanted Mark to vacate his store space early so he could start renovations. Mark refused."

"That is awful," Jenna said. "Mark loves that store. It has been in his family for years."

"Exactly," Ellie said. "Owen does not care about history unless he can sell it later at a profit. And that is not even the end of it. Someone else said he was seen leaving Harriet's office late last night. Harriet. The most organized, rule following woman in this entire valley. She does not stay late for anyone unless she is very angry or very convinced."

"Or both," Mara said.

"Yes," Ellie said. "There are rumors he threatened to withdraw sponsorship funds for the festival if she did not support one of his proposals."

"That man is exhausting," Jenna muttered.

Mara rubbed the back of her neck. "This feels like too many entanglements for one charity event."

"That is how Owen works," Ellie said. "He builds pressure. Everywhere he goes."

"Including here," Mara said quietly.

Ellie softened. "Just remember, you are not alone. You have people behind you. This bakery is part of the town's heart. He cannot push you around if the rest of us refuse to budge."

Before Mara could respond, Jenna lifted her camera again.

"Let me get a picture of you two," she said. "Smile like women who are absolutely not plotting to overthrow a tyrant."

Ellie gave a regal pose. Mara tried her best to look composed.

Two clicks later, Jenna checked her screen and nodded. "Perfect."

Mara tried to return to her work, but her gaze kept drifting to the front window. Something about the angle of the light and the reflection on the glass unsettled her. It was nothing obvious. Just a sensation. A whisper of movement where there should have been stillness.

She stepped closer.

Snow drifted past the window in lazy flakes. Across the street, the old bookstore sat quiet and still, its windows fogged from the owner's morning cooking. A few cars passed at a leisurely pace. A pair of children walked by with sleds, laughing as they kicked snow at each other.

No one suspicious. No shadows lingering. Nothing strange.

Yet she still felt watched.

"Mara?" Ellie called from the counter.

She blinked and turned back.

"Sorry," Mara said. "I thought I saw something."

Jenna stopped adjusting her camera. "Something like what?"

Mara hesitated.

"I am not sure," she said. "Probably nothing. Maybe just someone passing by."

"It is probably brunch nerves," Ellie said gently. "This is your first big event here. A little stress is normal."

"Maybe," Mara said.

But the feeling had not faded.

She tried to shake it off by diving back into the packaging process. She folded pastry boxes with renewed focus. She tied ribbons around snowflake cookies. She arranged the scones in neat lines inside the catering tray.

Ellie hummed contentedly beside her. Jenna snapped a few last pictures. The bakery brightened with movement again.

Still, every time Mara passed the window, her skin prickled.

The afternoon wore on. The trays filled and the counter emptied. The snow outside thickened, setting the stage for the kind of winter evening that begged for warm drinks and snug blankets.

"Almost done," Ellie said, stretching her arms. "This is more work than I expected."

"It is worth it," Mara said. "The brunch means a lot to the community."

"It does," Ellie agreed. "Still, I might sleep for three days after this is over."

"Same," Jenna said.

They shared a tired laugh and returned to their tasks.

Finally, everything sat packed and ready. The pastry boxes gleamed. The snowglobe was nestled in a cushioned crate. The bakery smelled like a festival of sugar and butter and joy.

Mara stood in the center of the room, hands on her hips.

"We did it," she said.

"Of course we did," Jenna said. "We are unstoppable."

Ellie tapped a folded box with her knuckles. "And your pastries look incredible. People are going to love them."

Mara felt a swell of quiet pride. "Thank you. Really."

She reached for one of the packed boxes and turned toward the counter.

Something caught her eye.

A shadow by the window.

She froze.

For a single breath, someone stood there. A figure. Still, watching, face hard to distinguish through the glare and snow. The outline was tall. Shouldered. Not moving.

Then it was gone.

Jenna noticed her go still. "What is it?"

"Someone was there," Mara whispered.

Ellie hurried to the window. "Where?"

Mara shook her head. "They moved. Or stepped back. I just saw the shape."

Jenna pressed both palms against the cold glass. "There is no one now."

"No," Mara said. "But they were."

Her heart thudded harder than the moment deserved. Maybe it had been a passerby. Maybe someone checking a phone. Maybe nothing.

But it felt like something.

Something connected to yesterday. Something she could not articulate but could not ignore.

Ellie slid her arm through Mara's.

"You are tired," she said. "And your imagination is being overproductive today. Let us finish cleaning and get you home. A little rest will help."

Mara nodded. "Maybe you are right."

They tidied the bakery. They stacked boxes. They labeled trays. They turned off the ovens and wiped the counters and swept the floors. Familiar motions, comforting motions. But the unease lingered in the background of Mara's mind like a low hum she could not shut off.

When the final light switched off and the bakery descended into its evening glow, the snow outside had thickened into a soft curtain.

Mara stood once more by the window.

Only the empty street greeted her.

Yet she could not shake the feeling that someone had been watching.

Someone who would not stay invisible for long.

Chapter 4

The Ice Pavilion glittered like a crystal lantern at the edge of
Frostberry Hollow.

Mara stood at the bottom of the shallow steps and took it in
for a moment, her breath curling in the cold air. The building
itself was not large, but the glass panels that framed its front
caught every scrap of winter light and threw it back in soft,
shimmering tones. Strings of white bulbs ran along the
roofline, already glowing faintly even though it was still
morning. Snowbanks hugged the path, neatly shoveled and
lined with evergreen branches.

Behind her, Ellie shifted the pastry box she carried.

"Stop holding your breath," Ellie said. "You will faint before the
doors even open."

"I am not holding my breath," Mara said.

"You are," Ellie replied. "I have known you long enough to
spot it."

Jenna, who balanced two boxes at once, nudged Mara with one elbow.

"Come on," Jenna said. "You have faced angry corporate executives and malfunctioning printers. You can handle a room full of townsfolk and a brunch buffet."

"That is a very low bar," Mara said. "Printers are scarier than most people."

"Well, there are no printers here," Jenna answered. "Only pastries, music and cheerful chaos."

"And gossip," Ellie added. "Do not forget the gossip."

Mara exhaled slowly and felt some of the tightness in her chest loosen.

"All right," she said. "Let us do this."

They climbed the steps together, careful to keep the boxes level. The glass doors swung open at their approach, the brass handles cool beneath Mara's fingers.

Inside, the world exploded into color and sound.

The main hall of the pavilion had been transformed. Round tables draped in white cloths filled the space, each one crowned with simple centerpieces of pine branches, cranberries in shallow glass bowls and small candles. At one end of the room, a raised platform held a clutch of musicians tuning their instruments. A violin sang a few bright notes. A cello hummed in reply. The air buzzed with the faint clatter of silverware, the squeak of chairs, the murmur of early arrivals.

Harriet Dove, chair of the brunch committee and unofficial queen of event planning, swept toward them with a clipboard in hand. Her hair was pinned in its usual meticulous twist, and her expression hovered between satisfaction and mild panic.

"You made it," she said, relief clear in her voice. "Thank goodness. The caterer for the egg dishes is late and I am two volunteers short for the raffle table. But at least you are here."

"We promised," Mara said.

Harriet eyed the boxes as if they were sacred cargo.

"Those are the gluten free scones?" she asked. "And the cinnamon rolls?"

"Yes," Mara said. "Gluten free here, regular there. The snowglobe is still in my car. I thought I would set the food up first and bring the globe in last."

"Good idea," Harriet said. "We do not want any accidents with that."

Her gaze warmed as it rested on Mara's face.

"You are doing the town a real favor," she added. "People look forward to these brunch treats more than you know."

Mara felt her cheeks flush.

"We are happy to help," she said.

Harriet pointed with her pen toward a long table near the center of the room.

"You are on the main buffet line," she said. "Right there between the fruit platters and the hot dishes. I wanted your pastries near the front so people cannot miss them."

"That seems like a lot of pressure," Mara muttered.

"Consider it a compliment," Ellie said under her breath.

They followed Harriet's direction and set the boxes on the indicated table. The white cloth draped to the floor, and someone had scattered paper snowflakes along the edges. Mara lifted the lids carefully. The scent of warm pastry rose at once, drifting into the larger room.

Several heads turned.

"See?" Jenna whispered. "You have already captured their attention."

Mara tried not to think about it too hard. She unpacked the trays, spreading them in neat rows, making sure the gluten free pastries were clearly separated and labeled. Ellie arranged small signs Harriet had provided, each one with beautiful looping script. Blackberry Scones. Cinnamon Rolls with Vanilla Glaze. Cranberry Scone Cake Slices. Gluten Free Blackberry Scones.

Harriet hovered nearby, ticking items off her list.

"Perfect," Harriet said. "Exactly what we needed. I knew I could count on you."

Her gaze shifted past Mara's shoulder.

"Mark," she called, her voice shifting into something brighter. "There you are. Come say hello."

Mara turned to see Mark Whitcomb weaving his way between tables. He wore a slightly rumpled button down shirt and a tie that looked like it had been chosen in the dark, but his smile was kind and his eyes carried a permanent hint of tiredness.

He owned the little home goods store that sat two doors down from the bakery. His family had run it for decades.

"Morning," Mark said, lifting a hand in greeting. "Smells fantastic in here."

"Thank you," Mara said. "We brought extra napkins in case people cry with joy."

"I might," Mark said with seriousness that made her laugh. Then his expression shifted. "Have you seen Owen yet?"

Mara's fingers tightened around the edge of the tray.

"Not yet," she said.

"Good," Mark muttered. "I could use a few minutes of peace before he starts making suggestions."

"Suggestions?" she asked.

"About the store," Mark said. "About everything. He thinks he knows how to improve the entire town. I am starting to think he would pave the creek if someone let him."

Harriet frowned and tapped her clipboard.

"We are not discussing Owen today," Harriet said. "At least not until after the fundraising total is announced. I would like to have one morning where people focus on generosity instead of bickering."

"You might be asking too much," Ellie said softly.

A voice cut through the noise behind them.

"You, my dear, are the one asking too much of me."

Tessa Barrow stepped into view, red coat flaring behind her, cheeks flushed from the cold. Her dark hair was braided over one shoulder, and she held a manila folder under one arm like a shield.

"I just spent twenty minutes arguing with the rental company," Tessa said. "They wanted to charge extra for chair covers. Chair covers. I told them the brunch committee did not budget for fabric that keeps people from seeing the chairs they are already using."

Harriet groaned softly. "Please tell me you did not shout at them."

"Of course I shouted at them," Tessa said. "That is what they understand."

She set the folder down and finally seemed to notice Mara fully.

"You must be the new baker," Tessa said. "Mara Linden. We met once in passing."

"We did," Mara said. "At the market."

"You made that gingerbread loaf that nearly made me cry," Tessa said. "I have been looking forward to this brunch for that reason alone."

"That might be the nicest review I have heard this week," Mara said.

"Believe it," Tessa replied. "And do not let Owen get to you, if he shows up. He has been in a mood."

"He always is in a mood," Mark muttered.

Tessa's jaw tightened.

Laughter and gentle chatter swelled around them as more guests arrived. Coats disappeared onto hooks. Gloves were stuffed into pockets. People greeted each other in warm bursts of sound that filled the space with comfort.

Mara finished setting out the last of the pastries and stepped back to look at the table. The scones sat in careful rows. The icing on the cinnamon rolls glistened under the lights. Everything looked ready.

Her heart rate finally started to slow.

"Could you two watch this for a moment?" she asked Ellie and Jenna. "I need to bring in the snowglobe."

"Of course," Jenna said. "Go fetch your masterpiece."

"Take your time," Ellie added. "We will guard the table from pastry thieves."

Mara unknotted her apron and folded it, leaving it beside the trays. She slipped through the clusters of people, offering quick smiles and nods, and stepped back into the cold.

Her car sat in the small parking lot behind the pavilion. She opened the trunk carefully. The snowglobe box was nestled between blankets to protect it from bumps and temperature shifts. She lifted it with both hands, feeling the familiar weight settle into her arms.

For a moment, she stood in the cold, watching her breath rise in thin curls.

Snowflakes brushed her hair and eyelashes. The world felt

strangely quiet here, just around the corner from all the laughter and music.

She carried the box back inside.

When she reentered the main hall, the noise rolled over her again. The musicians had started a gentle folk tune. People drifted from table to table, claiming seats and greeting neighbors. Children clustered near the back, whispering and giggling.

Harriet spotted her and hurried over.

"There it is," Harriet said, her eyes bright. "The star of the auction."

"I would not call it that," Mara said. "There are lots of nice things on the list."

Harriet lowered her voice.

"Between you and me," she said, "people love practical donations. Gift baskets, service vouchers, that sort of thing. But they are obsessed with one of a kind items. This snowglobe might start a bidding war."

"That sounds intense," Mara said.

"That sounds lucrative," Harriet replied. "And all the money goes to the clinic, so I am very comfortable with it."

Together, they carried the box to a small display table near the front of the room. The auction items were arranged there, each with a little card describing the donor and the item. A hand carved rocking chair. A weekend cabin stay. A handmade quilt. A basket of specialty teas.

Harriet cleared a space in the center and gestured grandly.

"Place it here," she said. "It deserves the spotlight."

Mara opened the box.

The glass caught the overhead light and pulsed with a soft glow. The tiny bridge gleamed faintly. The lamp at its center seemed to hold a miniature sun.

People nearby noticed at once.

"Oh," someone said. "Look at that."

"How lovely," another voice murmured.

Mara lifted the globe and set it gently on the display cloth. The movement of her hands sent the fake snow swirling inside, a gentle flurry that settled slowly over the scene.

"It looks like a memory," a woman said quietly.

"Or the start of one," someone else replied.

Mara stepped back, heart beating with a mix of pride and shyness.

She saw Mark watching from across the table, a faint smile on his face. Tessa stared, her expression unreadable. Even Harriet looked briefly overcome.

"It will do very well," Harriet said softly. "Thank you."

Before Mara could answer, the atmosphere in the room shifted.

A ripple passed through the crowd, subtle but noticeable. Conversations dipped. Heads turned toward the main entrance.

Mara followed their gaze.

Owen Barrow had arrived.

He stood in the doorway for a moment, snow clinging to the shoulders of his dark coat, jaw clenched. His eyes swept across the hall in a quick, calculating scan. Several people greeted him with cautious nods. Others looked away.

He moved forward, his steps precise and purposeful.

Mara felt her spine stiffen.

"Brace yourselves," Tessa muttered near her ear.

Owen crossed the room, offering greetings that sounded more like formal acknowledgments than genuine pleasantries. He shook hands with one council member, nodded at another, exchanged a curt phrase with the head of the clinic. Each interaction lasted only a beat before he moved on.

When he reached the auction table, his gaze landed on the snowglobe.

He stopped.

For a heartbeat, the room seemed to hush around him.

Then he stepped closer, expression reserved, eyes narrowing slightly.

"So this is the famous contribution," he said. "The one everyone has been talking about."

Mara resisted the urge to step between him and the globe like a guard dog.

"It is just a snowglobe," she said. "One of many items."

"It is not just a snowglobe," Owen replied. "People here are sentimental. They assign meaning to things. This is the sort of object that tempts them into bidding more than they can afford."

"There are worse uses for money than supporting the clinic," Harriet said crisply.

"True," Owen said. "As long as the funds are handled properly."

Harriet bristled but said nothing. The two of them stared at each other for a moment, tension crackling like static.

Owen looked at Mara again.

"You have done fine work," he said, in the same tone he might use to comment on a passable report. "It will pull attention. Perhaps too much."

"I consider that a compliment," Mara said.

"As you wish."

He turned away, his gaze already sliding toward the cluster of local officials near the far wall.

On instinct, Mara watched him as he moved through the room.

He paused to speak with a council member, his posture close and intense. The council member's smile looked strained. Then Owen stepped away, brushing past a knot of guests, exchanging a polite remark here and there. Each interaction seemed to leave a faint wake of discomfort behind him.

He was a man who disturbed the air wherever he walked.

Mara tried to refocus on the buffet, but she could not stop tracking his progress with the corner of her eye.

At one point, she lost sight of him entirely.

"Where did he go?" she murmured.

"Who?" Ellie asked.

"Owen," Mara said.

Ellie scanned the room. "He was near the back a moment ago."

"I do not see him now."

"Maybe he stepped into the hall," Ellie suggested. "Or into the kitchen."

Mara's attention caught on a narrow doorway near the side of the room. It led to a small hallway that ran behind the main hall, connecting the kitchen, coatroom and utility closets. The door itself sat partly in shadow, the light from the main area unable to reach fully into its frame.

For a moment, she saw movement there.

A figure lingered near the doorway, just inside the dim hall. Owen stood close, his back partly turned toward the main room. He leaned in, speaking to someone obscured by the doorframe. The other person's outline was indistinct. A shoulder. A sleeve. The hint of a hat.

Mara squinted, trying to make sense of the shapes.

Owen's posture was tense. His hand lifted in a sharp gesture. The shadowed figure did not move much, but something about their stillness felt deliberate.

"Ellie," Mara said quietly.

Ellie followed her gaze.

"What is it?" Ellie asked.

"Look," Mara said. "By the side hallway. Do you see them?"

Ellie peered more closely.

"I see Owen," she said. "I cannot make out the other person."

"They are arguing," Mara whispered. "I think."

The music from the stage swelled, masking any words. Guests shifted between the tables, blocking parts of Mara's view in brief flickers. She stepped to the side for a clearer line of sight, but in that instant, the figures separated.

Owen stepped fully into view again, jaw set, eyes colder than ever. He moved away from the doorway without looking back. The shadow in the hall retreated further into the dimness and disappeared from her view.

"Did you see who it was?" Mara asked.

"No," Ellie said. "Only the shape."

"Tall," Mara said. "Or they were standing on something. I could not tell."

Ellie glanced at her.

"Could have been anyone," she said. "Kitchen staff. A volunteer. A council member."

"Or someone who does not want to be seen," Mara said softly.

A strange unease settled in her stomach. Not the flutter of nerves she had felt before the event. Something darker. Something that whispered of secrets traded in the edges of the room.

On the stage, the musicians shifted into a brighter tune. Harriet clapped her hands for attention and called out a cheerful welcome. People turned toward her, smiling, ready to begin.

Mara straightened her shoulders and smoothed the front of her dress.

"Time to work," she said.

"Time to impress," Jenna added, appearing at her side with the camera ready.

"Time," Ellie said, "to see what the new year really has in store for us."

They moved to their stations as the brunch officially began, unaware that a single plate of pastries and a quiet conversation in a shadowed hallway would alter the course of the day, and their lives, in ways none of them could yet imagine.

Chapter 5

The brunch reached its warm and bustling rhythm within minutes.

Laughter drifted across the Ice Pavilion in gentle waves. Chairs scraped against the polished floor. Plates clinked softly. A winter sun filtered through the glass panels overhead, touching the tables with a faint golden shimmer that made the pine centerpiece decorations glow.

Mara stood behind her pastry display, hands folded lightly at her waist, watching people approach the buffet. Guests sampled fruit, spooned eggs onto plates, and paused thoughtfully in front of her pastries before choosing one. The sight should have comforted her, and in many ways it did.

These were her recipes. Her creations. Little pieces of warmth she had worked tirelessly to perfect.

Jenna circled the room with her camera, capturing the morning from smooth angles. Ellie stood near the raffle table, handing out tickets with a smile that never seemed to fade.

Mara inhaled the combined scents of cinnamon, berries, citrus and warm bread. The music from the stage floated across the tables in a soft, inviting melody.

For the first time all morning, she let herself relax.

People were enjoying themselves. Guests chatted with neighbors. Several complimented the pastries directly to her, thanking her for the gluten free options and the fresh fruit glazes. A few even asked for recipes or offered stories about her aunt Iris.

It was the kind of community moment she had always hoped to be part of.

She spotted Mark loading his plate with cautious enthusiasm while muttering to himself about calories. Tessa stood near a group of teachers, gesturing animatedly as she spoke. Harriet floated between guests like a conductor, ensuring every detail remained perfect.

Mara allowed a small sigh of contentment.

Maybe everything would be all right today.

Maybe she could enjoy this.

Her gaze traveled across the long buffet table and paused when Owen Barrow stepped into view again.

He moved with a stiff, purposeful stride, his coat discarded somewhere, his shirt pressed so sharply it seemed to resist wrinkling. His expression remained unreadable but slightly pinched, as if the brightness of the morning annoyed him on principle.

He reached the buffet line with barely a greeting. People stepped aside for him instinctively, their smiles fading to polite small ones.

Mara tried not to stiffen.

Jenna, passing nearby, shot her a sympathetic glance before focusing on the musicians again.

Mara straightened the pastry tongs and waited.

Owen lifted a plate from the stack, his movements impatient. He spooned eggs onto his plate, ignored the fruit entirely, and reached the pastry section.

His eyes landed on the gluten free scones, the very ones he had mocked the previous morning.

He hesitated for half a second. Then he picked one up.

Mara felt her breath catch in her throat.

She reminded herself he was simply another guest. Simply someone attending the brunch. Nothing more. No matter his sharp words and colder stare, he was not a threat to a tray of pastries.

Still, she watched him.

He brought the scone to his mouth.

Took a bite.

Chewed.

His expression did not change. It remained impassive, unreadable. He swallowed, lifted his fork, and moved as though reaching for something else.

Then he froze.

Only for a heartbeat. But enough for Mara's stomach to twist.

His hand trembled.

The fork slid from his grasp and clattered against his plate.

He opened his mouth slightly, as if to speak. No sound came.

His knees buckled.

Someone nearby gasped.

Owen fell forward, bracing reflexively with one hand before collapsing fully onto the polished floor.

A plate shattered. Eggs scattered in a messy splash.

For a second the room was silent.

Then chaos.

Voices rose in startled cries. Chairs scraped back as people lurched to their feet. A woman near the fruit platters covered her mouth with both hands. Someone else shouted for help. The musicians stopped abruptly, the final note cutting off in a jarring break.

Mara stood frozen, her body refusing to move.

Jenna lowered her camera with a shaky hand and stared. Ellie hurried forward, her face pale.

Harriet dropped her clipboard and crouched beside Owen, calling his name twice. There was no response.

"He is not breathing," someone whispered.

"Call the clinic," another said. "Now."

A man pulled his phone from his pocket and dialed. Guests gathered in a loose, frightened circle.

Mara forced her body to take a step forward. Then another. Her hands felt cold, colder than the snow outside the pavilion.

She reached Harriet's side.

"Is he...?" Mara asked, her voice barely a whisper.

"We do not know," Harriet managed. "He just collapsed."

Owen lay still, his skin drained of color, a faint bluish tone settling around his mouth. One half eaten scone rested next to his hand on the floor.

Her scone.

A sharp sound cracked the air.

The pavilion doors swung open. A figure hurried in, boots crunching on the thin trail of slush left behind by early guests.

Sheriff Connor Hale.

His presence shifted the energy of the room at once. People stepped back automatically, giving him space.

Connor moved with practiced calm, though Mara noticed the tension across his jaw. He approached Harriet first, then knelt to check Owen. His fingers found the man's neck, searching.

Harriet held her breath.

Mara held hers too.

Connor looked up after a long moment.

"He is gone," he said quietly.

A collective shudder passed through the crowd.

Several guests turned away, murmuring prayers or pressing their hands to their mouths. Someone hurried toward the stage, perhaps seeking privacy from sudden grief.

Connor stood slowly and faced the room.

"Everyone remain where you are," he said. "Do not leave yet."

Mara felt the words land inside her chest like a blow.

The sheriff's gaze swept the floor, taking in the fallen plate, the scone crumbs, the pastry trays.

Then his eyes met hers.

"Mara," he said. "I need you to step over here."

Her stomach dropped.

She approached, her hands trembling.

"Is this your tray?" he asked, gesturing to the gluten free pastries.

"Yes," she whispered.

"And this is one of your scones?"

"Yes."

Connor studied her, his expression unreadable.

"Until we understand what happened," he said, "I am taking these into custody."

Her breath caught.

"But… they are just scones," she said. "There is nothing in them."

"I am not saying otherwise," Connor replied. "This is procedure."

He gestured for one of the officers who had arrived behind him. The officer lifted the entire tray carefully, placing it inside a sealed container.

Mara stared, numb.

The room felt too warm. Too bright. Too loud, even though no one was speaking loudly anymore.

Ellie reached her and placed a gentle hand on her arm. "Breathe," Ellie whispered. "Just breathe."

Jenna hovered close, her face pale. "This is not your fault," she whispered fiercely.

But Mara barely heard them.

Her gaze drifted toward the auction table.

A shiver ran through her.

The snowglobe.

The New Beginnings globe she had placed so carefully earlier.

It was gone.

Not moved. Not shifted. Gone.

The table where it had sat displayed a small empty space between the rocking chair and the quilt, the card describing the snowglobe still propped upright, alone.

She grabbed Jenna's sleeve.

"The snowglobe," Mara said, her voice cracking. "It is missing."

Jenna spun. "What? No. It was right there."

"It is gone," Mara said. "Someone took it."

Connor heard her and turned toward the auction table, his attention sharpening.

"Are you certain?" he asked.

"Yes," Mara said. "I set it there myself. It was the centerpiece. It is gone."

Connor took a long, steady breath, then motioned to another officer.

"Check the exits," he said. "Ask anyone standing near that table what they saw."

Guests murmured in confusion. Several looked toward Mara with expressions she could not read. Sympathy. Curiosity. Fear. Doubt.

Everything blurred at the edges.

Connor returned to her.

"Mara," he said, softer now, "I know this is overwhelming. But I need you to come with me for a few questions."

Her throat tightened.

Ellie stepped forward. "She is shaken," Ellie said firmly. "Let her breathe."

"I will," Connor said. "But right now, I need information while memories are fresh."

Mara nodded, though she felt half detached from her own body.

Owen's collapse.

Her scone tray sealed away.

Her snowglobe missing.

The shadowed figure in the hallway.

A chill slid down her spine.

Nothing about this morning made sense anymore.

Connor guided her gently toward a quieter corner of the pavilion, away from the spreading circle of fear and speculation.

Behind her, the brunch continued in shocked whispers.

Mara felt every step like moving through cold water.

Whatever had just unfolded, she was no longer simply a baker preparing for a charity event.

She was at the center of something she did not yet understand.

* * *

Connor guided Mara toward a smaller alcove at the edge of the pavilion, where a decorative pine tree blocked most of the view from the main hall. The quiet there felt strangely heavy, muffled by layers of shock and fear that hung in the air like low fog.

"Sit if you need to," Connor said, keeping his voice low so it would not carry.

Mara shook her head. "Standing is better. If I sit, I may not get up again."

Connor studied her carefully, his steady presence somehow grounding.

"I know this is frightening," he said. "But I need to ask a few questions while everything is fresh."

Mara nodded, though her heart thudded hard enough that she could feel it in her fingertips.

Connor pulled a small notebook from his pocket.

"When did you last check the gluten free scones before Owen took one?" he asked.

"Just a few minutes before he arrived," she said. "I straightened the trays, made sure the signs were placed clearly. Nothing looked wrong."

"You watched him take the scone?" Connor asked.

"Yes," Mara said. "He picked it up with the tongs. I watched him take a bite."

"And before that," Connor said, "did you see anyone approach that tray? Anyone who might have touched it?"

Mara tried to rewind her memory. She closed her eyes for a moment, letting the scene settle.

"I saw a few guests near it," she said. "A couple with a stroller, then two teenagers. They looked at the sign but walked past. No one touched anything."

"No one lingered?" Connor asked.

She paused.

"Not that I noticed," she said. "It was busy. People were talking. I was talking."

Connor nodded slowly.

"Your pastries were prepared this morning?" he asked.

"Yes," Mara said, feeling a twist in her stomach. "Fresh. I have been working for hours. Ellie helped me package everything. Jenna photographed things. Nothing odd happened."

Connor considered this.

"There is no suspicion toward you," he said firmly. "I want you to hear that. This is a routine step."

Mara tried to smile, but her mouth would not cooperate.

"That routine step involves taking my tray away," she said.

Connor exhaled softly.

"Yes," he said. "I need to test everything. This may have nothing to do with the food at all. His collapse could have been caused by a medical issue. But we do not assume anything."

Her mind raced.

"What about his expression?" she asked. "Before he fell. He looked... strange."

"Strange how?" Connor prompted.

Mara searched for words.

"Like something hit him all at once," she said. "Shock. Pain. I do not know. It was quick."

Connor jotted something down.

"And the snowglobe?" he asked. "When did you last see it?"

"Before the collapse," Mara said. "Maybe twenty minutes before. Harriet and I placed it at the center of the auction table. People admired it."

"And no one saw who removed it?" he asked.

"I do not think so," Mara said. "But the table was busy. People kept walking around it. Someone could have taken it quickly."

Connor nodded, face tightening.

"I will put out a notice and check the exits," he said. "For now, we focus on what we know."

Mara swallowed.

"What do we know?" she asked quietly.

Connor hesitated for a moment.

"We know Owen Barrow collapsed in a room full of witnesses," he said. "We know he ate part of one of your pastries, but that does not mean it caused anything. We also know something was stolen. That suggests intention."

Her chest tightened.

"Do you think these things are connected?" she asked.

Connor's voice was careful when he answered.

"I do not know yet," he said. "But I intend to find out as quickly as possible."

Mara pressed a hand against her forehead, trying to steady herself. Her thoughts were spinning. The warmth of the pavilion felt suffocating despite the cold air outside.

"I should… I should help clean," she said weakly. "Or check on Ellie. Or find Jenna."

Connor shook his head.

"You need air," he said. "You are pale. Go outside for a moment. Ellie can handle things here."

"I cannot just leave," she protested.

"You will be back," Connor said gently. "Five minutes. Ten at most. I need you steady, and right now you are shaking."

She looked down.

He was right. Her hands trembled faintly, like a soft vibration she could not stop.

"All right," she said.

Connor signaled to Ellie, who hurried over, her face etched with worry.

"Take her outside," Connor said quietly. "Not far. Just until she can breathe again."

Ellie wrapped an arm around Mara's shoulders.

"Come on," Ellie said gently. "I will stay with you."

Mara let herself be guided toward a side door. The cold hit them instantly, sharp and clear. It stung her cheeks but also cut through the fog in her head.

They stepped onto the small patio at the side of the pavilion. Snowflakes drifted lazily from a pale sky. The quiet out here felt unreal after the chaos inside.

Mara leaned against the railing, gripping it with both hands.

"I do not understand," she whispered. "It happened so fast."

"You did nothing wrong," Ellie said firmly. "Do not let fear convince you of something that is not true."

"But the scone," Mara said. "The snowglobe. It is all connected somehow."

"We do not know that," Ellie said. "Not yet."

Mara stared at the snow-covered bushes below the railing.

"I feel responsible," she whispered.

"You are not," Ellie repeated. "Other people's secrets and decisions are not your fault, even if they brush close to your life."

The words should have comforted her.

But something heavy still pressed against her chest.

"Ellie," she said. "The snowglobe is gone."

"I know," Ellie said quietly. "That part... that part is strange."

"I think someone watched the bakery yesterday," Mara whispered. "I saw a shadow outside. Then today it goes missing."

Ellie's grip tightened.

"I do not like that," Ellie said. "Not at all."

They stood there for a long moment, listening to the soft whisper of falling snow.

Finally, Ellie exhaled.

"You need to go home," she said. "Connor can handle things here. Jenna will find us later."

"I cannot just leave," Mara said faintly.

"I know," Ellie said. "But you are not helping anyone by collapsing yourself. And you look ready to."

Mara closed her eyes.

"Fine," she whispered. "Just for an hour."

Ellie nodded.

"I will walk you to your car."

The short walk around the pavilion felt unreal. The snow muted all sound. Each step crunched softly under their boots. Mara kept glancing over her shoulder, half expecting to see a shadow lurking between the trees or near the glass windows.

But the world remained still.

They reached her car. Mara unlocked it with shaking hands.

"You will call me when you get home?" Ellie asked.

"Yes," Mara said. "I promise."

"And you will not blame yourself for this?"

Mara hesitated.

"I will try."

Ellie hugged her tightly.

"Good," Ellie said. "That is enough for now."

Mara climbed into the car. The cold interior wrapped around her like a sigh. She started the engine and sat for a moment, gripping the wheel.

The image of Owen collapsing replayed in her mind again. And again.

Then the empty space where her snowglobe had been.

Her breath trembled.

She pulled out of the parking lot slowly, watching the pavilion recede in the rearview mirror.

Something in that building had gone terribly wrong.

And Mara could not shake the terrible thought forming in her mind.

Someone had planned it.

Someone had stolen her snowglobe.

Someone had been watching.

She drove home through the falling snow, unaware that the mystery now circling her life had already begun to close in.

Chapter 6

The next morning arrived slow and gray, the kind of winter morning that felt reluctant to begin. A soft fog settled over Frostberry Hollow, clinging to rooftops and drifting low through the narrow streets. The town looked half awake, its edges blurred by the lingering quiet after yesterday's shock.

Inside the Cozy Nook Bakery, Mara stood behind the counter, twisting a cloth napkin between her fingers. She had opened on time, as usual. The ovens hummed. The scent of cinnamon and warm dough filled the air. A row of fresh pastries lined the display case. Everything looked the same.

But nothing felt the same.

The bell above the door chimed for the first time that morning, and Mara flinched before she could stop herself.

A middle aged woman stepped inside, brushing snow from her shoulders. She hesitated, almost imperceptibly, before approaching the pastry case. Her gaze flicked to Mara, then to the scones, then back again.

"Morning," Mara said gently.

The woman offered a tight smile. "Morning."

She scanned the options again, biting her lower lip. After a long pause, she pointed at a cinnamon roll.

"Just that," she said.

"Of course," Mara replied.

She placed the pastry in a paper bag, set it on the counter, and rang up the total. The woman paid quickly, avoided eye contact, and left with a murmured thank you.

The bell chimed again.

Mara exhaled slowly.

A few minutes later, an older couple entered. They were regulars who usually chatted with her about weather and grandkids and recipes they wanted to try at home. Today, they whispered to each other near the tables, glancing toward the counter more than once.

They eventually ordered two coffees and nothing else.

Then they left.

The pattern repeated again and again.

People walked in. Paused. Whispered. Bought coffee, tea, maybe a plain roll or a muffin. But not one person ordered a scone. Not one person reached for anything resembling what Owen Barrow had eaten yesterday.

By mid morning, Mara's chest felt tight.

She stood behind the counter wiping the same spot on the countertop long after it was clean.

A pair of teenagers near the front window spoke softly, unaware she could hear them.

"I told you," one said, "it was the scone."

"You do not know that," the other whispered.

"My mom said everyone at the brunch thinks so."

"That is not fair," the friend replied.

"It is what people are saying."

Mara closed her eyes.

The bell chimed again.

Connor Hale stepped inside.

He removed his hat and brushed snow from his coat as he approached the counter. His expression was neither warm nor cold. Measured. Professional.

"Morning," he said.

"Morning," Mara replied, trying to sound composed.

"Can we talk?" he asked.

She nodded and led him to a small table in the corner, away from the other customers. She wiped her hands on her apron and sat, though her nerves screamed for her to stand.

Connor rested his hat on the table and intertwined his fingers.

"I know this is difficult," he said quietly. "I wanted to stop by before the day gets too far along."

"You can tell me," Mara said. "Whatever it is. Please."

Connor paused before answering. "We are still waiting on results."

Mara's stomach twisted.

"I understand," she said. "You are testing the scones."

"We are testing everything," Connor said. "Food samples. Plates. Utensils. Anything that may have come into contact with Owen before he collapsed."

"Does that mean you think something was poisoned?" Mara asked.

Connor did not answer immediately.

"We are not ruling anything out yet," he said. "Which is why I cannot share too much. I do not want to mislead you or the town."

"But people already assume it was the scone," Mara whispered.

"I know."

"They are avoiding the pastries. They are whispering."

Connor's gaze softened.

"People cling to simple explanations when they are scared," he said. "It does not mean they are right."

"It does not mean they are wrong either," Mara replied, voice trembling.

Connor studied her for a long moment.

"Do you trust your own recipes?" he asked.

"Yes," she said immediately. "Absolutely."

"Then trust them now," he said.

Mara swallowed hard. "What am I supposed to do? Just wait?"

"For now," Connor said gently. "I promise you, the moment I learn anything definitive, you will know."

He rose from his chair.

"I will check in again later," he said. "Try to take care of yourself."

"Thank you," Mara said quietly.

He nodded, placed his hat back on his head, and left the bakery.

The door closed behind him.

The bell chimed faintly.

Mara sat alone for several seconds before she could breathe again.

A soft rustling sounded near the back of the shop.

"Mara?" Ellie's voice floated from the kitchen doorway.

Mara turned.

Ellie stepped out, wiping her hands on a towel, her expression heavy with concern. A moment later, Jenna followed, camera bag still slung over her shoulder, hair pulled back as if she had rushed over the moment she woke.

"We heard what people are saying," Jenna said, keeping her voice low. "And we are not letting you deal with this alone."

Ellie sat beside Mara, placing a warm hand over hers. "What did Connor say?"

"He is testing everything," Mara said. "He will not say whether they suspect foul play, but they are not ruling it out."

Jenna let out a breath. "Of course people are jumping to conclusions. It is easier than thinking something complicated happened."

Ellie squeezed Mara's hand. "Listen to me. You are not responsible for whatever happened to Owen Barrow. Even if someone used your pastries, that does not make it your fault."

"But the bakery," Mara whispered. "If people lose trust in us... if they stop coming..."

She could not finish the sentence.

Her throat tightened too much.

Jenna leaned forward. "This town needs your bakery. It needs a place to gather and talk and share things. It needs you."

"I do not know if that is enough," Mara said.

"It is," Ellie said firmly. "We will face this. One day at a time."

Customers came and went quietly, their whispers filling the space the moment they thought Mara could not hear.

Ellie stayed near the front, stepping in when people hesitated. She made gentle conversation, insisted the coffee was fresh, and handed out small complimentary sugar cookies without asking for payment.

Jenna arranged some pastries near the window, adjusting everything so it looked inviting and warm.

Still, the unease did not lift.

By late afternoon, the bakery grew quiet again. Snow fell outside in soft, wandering flakes. The lights inside glowed against the dimness, creating a cozy space that should have felt comforting.

Mara stood in the center of the bakery and looked around. The room felt familiar yet fragile, as if a single hard wind could sweep everything out from under her.

She walked to the snowglobe cabinet and rested her hand against the glass.

Aunt Iris had believed this place could be a home. A safe corner of the world. A place built on laughter and warmth and sugar dusted mornings.

Mara closed her eyes.

"I will not lose this," she whispered.

The words felt like a promise spoken into the quiet air.

A vow to herself.

A vow to her aunt.

A vow to the small, steady hope she had carried with her since the day she stepped into Frostberry Hollow.

"I will protect this bakery," she whispered again. "No matter what it takes."

Her voice trembled. But the promise held.

Outside, the snow thickened.

Inside, Mara stood alone with her vow, unaware that the mystery surrounding Owen's death would tighten in the days ahead, pulling her deeper into a world of secrets the town had hidden for years.

Chapter 7

The next morning arrived with clear skies and a thin layer of glittering frost on the bakery windows. The sunlight looked deceptively bright, as if the world outside were peaceful and simple. Mara knew better now. Quiet mornings no longer felt innocent. They felt like a pause before the next piece of truth revealed itself.

She was restocking the pastry case when the bell above the door chimed.

Jenna stumbled in, cheeks pink from the cold, curls escaping her hat in every direction. She held her camera bag like it was priceless cargo and kicked the snow off her boots with hurried urgency.

"You need to see this," Jenna said, skipping any greeting.

"What is it?" Mara straightened at once.

Jenna marched to a corner table and plopped her camera bag down. She dragged out her laptop and powered it on.

"You took more pictures yesterday?" Mara asked.

"I always take more pictures than necessary," Jenna replied, tapping impatiently at the keyboard. "Most of them are terrible. Blurry. People chewing. Mystery elbows. But sometimes I catch something unexpected."

She opened a file labeled Brunch Candids.

Rows of thumbnails filled the screen.

Mara pulled a chair beside her. "Where are these from?"

"Moments before everything went wrong," Jenna said quietly. "I was taking crowd shots. Trying to capture the energy of the room. And... I accidentally caught something else."

She clicked one thumbnail.

The image opened.

Mara leaned closer.

It showed a cluster of guests near the center of the Ice Pavilion. Music stands in the background, people milling around, lifts of bright conversation frozen in stillness.

But in the left corner of the frame... Owen Barrow stood slightly turned away, his posture tense.

He was reaching for an envelope.

A gloved hand extended it.

A hand that did not belong to anyone visible in full.

"Zoom in," Mara whispered.

Jenna did.

The image blurred slightly but held enough detail to see the exchange clearly. Owen's fingers gripped the envelope. The other hand, partly hidden behind a corner post, appeared in a dark glove with a black button at the wrist. The sleeve above it was thick winter fabric, wool or felt, dark charcoal in color.

The body connected to the hand was mostly out of frame.

But the shape was visible enough to know two things.

It was not a child.

It was not elderly.

Someone in between.

"Mara," Jenna said softly, "I did not even notice this when I was taking the photos. But look at Owen's face."

Mara focused.

Owen's features were tight, concentrated, a shade colder than usual. His jaw clenched. His eyes fixed on the envelope as if he already knew what was inside.

"Do you remember seeing him receive anything?" Jenna asked.

"No," Mara said, her stomach turning. "I saw him moving through the room, but I missed this."

Jenna clicked forward to the next photo.

It showed the same corner, but the gloved figure was gone. Owen stood alone, slipping the envelope into his inside coat pocket.

The timestamp in the corner read just twelve minutes before his collapse.

Mara's fingers curled around the edge of the table.

"Someone gave him something," she said. "Something he hid."

"And twelve minutes later he fell," Jenna added quietly.

Mara stared at the screen without blinking.

"What did we miss?" she whispered.

Jenna shook her head. "I do not know. But this proves something else was happening. Something no one talked about."

She clicked through two more photos. Each showed pieces of the room. Decorations. Buffet tables. People smiling. And then...

"There," Mara whispered, pointing.

The dark sleeve.

The gloved hand. Again.

Not close to Owen this time, but near the side hallway where she had seen the shadowy figure.

"Well I do not like that," Jenna murmured.

"Neither do I," Mara said.

The sleeve looked the same. The glove looked the same. The posture was similar. A quiet observer standing where most guests did not linger.

Jenna scrolled again.

Another blurred image. Partial. Difficult. But the same figure, half turned, only the curve of a shoulder visible, as if avoiding full capture.

"Who is that?" Jenna whispered.

"We need Ellie," Mara said.

Jenna closed the laptop. "Let us get her."

The bell chimed again as they turned, and Ellie entered as if summoned.

She took one look at their faces and stopped mid step.

"What happened?" Ellie asked, setting down her canvas bag.

"Come here," Jenna said. "You need to see the photos."

Ellie removed her gloves and joined them at the table. Mara reopened the laptop and replayed the sequence, letting Ellie absorb each detail.

Ellie's brows furrowed.

"That is definitely an envelope," Ellie said. "And that glove... I recognize the button style."

"You do?" Mara asked.

"Half the town wears knitted mittens," Ellie said. "Only a few people wear lined gloves with buttons like that. And that sleeve is not cheap. That is layered winter wool, not something you find at the discount rack."

Jenna leaned forward. "Who do you think it is?"

Ellie did not answer right away.

She tapped her finger lightly against her chin, thinking.

"It might narrow the list," Ellie said slowly. "But we need more clues before pointing fingers."

Mara felt a tremor of frustration beneath her ribs.

"I cannot stop thinking about the snowglobe," she said. "Someone took it. Someone who knew exactly when to act. What if these things are connected?"

Ellie's expression turned thoughtful.

"Mara," Ellie said, "what if the snowglobe contained something?"

Mara blinked. "What do you mean?"

"Think about it," Ellie said. "Your aunt made snowglobes for years. She built secret compartments into several of them. She always said they could hold tiny messages or charms."

Mara felt something in her chest twist.

"You think someone hid something in mine?"

"It is possible," Ellie said gently. "Or they thought something was hidden inside. If someone wanted the snowglobe badly enough, maybe they believed it held answers to whatever Owen was dealing with."

Jenna nodded slowly. "And if Owen met someone in secret before he collapsed, they might have been looking for the same thing."

Mara swallowed. "But why take my snowglobe when the envelope already existed?"

"We do not know," Ellie said. "Maybe the envelope was not enough. Maybe the snowglobe was the real prize."

A quiet settled over them.

Then Jenna straightened, resolve sparking in her eyes.

"Well," Jenna said, "if the sheriff is busy testing food samples and waiting for lab results, someone should look into this from our side."

"You mean us?" Mara asked.

"Yes," Jenna said. "Us."

Ellie crossed her arms. "We are sensible, grown adults. We will not do anything reckless."

"Of course not," Jenna replied. Then she grinned. "Just smart."

Mara stared at the photo of the gloved hand again.

The dark sleeve.

The button at the wrist.

The hidden face.

The envelope.

A new resolve began to form inside her, growing slowly but steadily, like a small flame fed by cold air.

"Owen received something important," Mara said. "Something

private. Something someone else cared about enough to take my snowglobe for."

"And maybe enough to do worse," Ellie added softly.

Mara nodded.

"Then we follow the clues," she said.

Jenna reached for her camera bag like it was a shield.

"And we start today," Jenna said. "Before whoever that is decides to move again."

Ellie gave a reluctant but accepting sigh.

"Fine," she said. "But we stay together. No wandering off alone. If someone took your snowglobe, they might not stop there."

Mara closed the laptop.

The bakery seemed different now. Less quiet. Less cozy. Shadows in the corners felt heavier. The snow outside the window looked colder.

She looked at her friends.

"Let us find the truth," she said.

And for the first time since the brunch, she felt the faintest spark of control returning.

A small spark.

Fragile.

But real.

Chapter 8

The Old Mill Market always felt like stepping into another world. Even on the coldest winter mornings, warmth poured from the tall brick building that had once housed water wheels and grinding stones. Now its rooms held vendor stalls, bakeries, butcher counters, craft displays and shelves of goods from local farms. Every visit smelled of roasted nuts, citrus peels, spices and the faint smokiness of cured meats.

Mara pushed through the creaking double doors, grateful for the sudden heat that washed over her. It hugged her like a familiar blanket after the cold walk. Voices echoed through the cavernous interior, blending with the hum of conversation and the crisp shuffle of shoppers' boots on the worn wooden floors.

She pulled her coat tighter and scanned the main aisle.

People milled between the stalls, bundled in heavy scarves, puffing little clouds of breath as they talked. Children darted between their parents' legs. A vendor offered mulled cider samples. The entire place carried that particular winter magic that felt equal parts festive and comforting.

Mara wished she could enjoy it.

But ever since the brunch, the market felt like a room filled with hidden thoughts. Conversations dipped when she walked by, then rose again as she moved on. People tried to smile politely, but too many glances lingered a bit too long, curious or cautious or unsure.

She forced herself to breathe through the nerves tightening her chest.

She was here for answers.

Tessa's booth was near the back. Fresh flowers were still part of her display, though winter limited her selection to greenery, seed bundles and dried arrangements. Still, her stall stood out in a cheerful burst of life among jars of pickles, rows of honey and rustic handmade crafts.

Tessa herself stood behind the counter, sorting a box of dried lavender stems. Her hair was pulled back tightly, and her expression was more strained than the last time Mara had seen her.

"Mara," Tessa said when she noticed her approaching. "You came alone. Brave woman."

"I needed a change of scenery," Mara said lightly. "And I had a few questions, if you have a moment."

Tessa huffed with a faint laugh. "Questions. Everyone has questions after yesterday."

She gestured to the lavender with a dramatic sweep. "Ask away. I am already surrounded by calming herbs. I will pretend they work."

Mara stepped closer.

"Your land," Mara said. "You mentioned Owen tried to buy it."

Tessa's jaw tightened immediately.

"He did not try," she said. "He pushed. And pushed. And pushed."

"What did he want with it?" Mara asked.

"That is the mystery," Tessa said. "He claimed he wanted to use it for storage or a seasonal warehouse. But it made no sense. I know what that property is worth. And I know what a warehouse brings in. He was not being honest."

"What do you think he really wanted?"

Tessa leaned her elbows on the counter, voice lowering.

"There is an old well on my land," she said. "Sealed decades ago. People say it connects to a series of underground tunnels from the mining days. Owen asked about that well repeatedly. Too many times."

Mara shivered.

"You think he was after something down there?"

"I think he believed something was," Tessa said. "Maybe documents. Maybe valuables. Who knows. He had a knack for digging into Frostberry Hollow history when it suited him."

"Did you argue about it recently?" Mara asked.

Tessa laughed without warmth.

"Yesterday morning," she said. "Before the brunch. He told me I would regret holding on to land that should have been sold years ago. I told him he needed a good nap and a warm meal."

"Did he threaten you?"

Tessa shook her head. "Not directly. Owen never threatens outright. He wraps his threats in phrasing that sounds like financial advice. But his meaning is clear."

Mara considered this.

"Are you all right?" she asked softly.

Tessa paused, surprising Mara with the slight tremor that passed through her expression.

"I do not know," Tessa admitted. "I did not like him. But I did not want him dead."

Mara nodded. "I understand."

Tessa straightened again, shoving her emotions back into place with a practiced motion.

"You are not here to blame me," she said. "So go find the person who deserves it."

Mara moved on through the market, her mind buzzing with the new information. Owen had wanted Tessa's land for something beneath it. A hidden well. Possibly tunnels. That piece settled heavily in her thoughts.

She continued through the aisles until she reached Mark Whitcomb's corner stall. Rustic wooden shelves held rows of handmade soaps and candles from the back of his shop. Mark himself stood hunched over a crate, sorting inventory with the focus of someone trying to work through stress.

He looked up when Mara approached.

"Oh," he said. "Hi."

"Hi," Mara said gently. "I hope this is a good time."

"As good as any," Mark said. "No one is buying anything today. People are too busy discussing what happened at the brunch."

Mara nodded.

"You said you and Owen argued," she said quietly.

Mark's shoulders sagged.

"Yes," he said. "We did."

"Why?"

Mark set down a candle jar with a thud.

"He was trying to push me out," Mark said. "The building my store is in, he has been trying to buy it for months. I refused to sell. So he raised my rent. Twice. Then he told me he would give me one last chance to accept his offer before he started formal eviction proceedings."

"He cannot evict you without cause," Mara said.

"He thinks not selling to him is cause," Mark said bitterly. "He always frames things that way."

"Did you see him on the morning of the brunch?" Mara asked.

"Yes," Mark said. "He stopped by the market early. Tried again to convince me to sell. I told him no. He told me I was making a mistake."

Mark swallowed hard.

"I am not proud of it," he said. "But I snapped. I told him if he wanted to dig around in town history so badly, he could bury himself in it."

Mara touched his arm gently. "That sounds like a moment of frustration, not a threat."

"Does it?" Mark asked quietly. "Because I am afraid other people heard it differently."

She shook her head. "You are not responsible for what happened."

Mark let out a sad, brittle sigh.

"I wish that were easier to believe," he said.

Mara stayed with him another minute before stepping away. The market felt heavier now. She sensed the tension not only between the vendors but in the air itself, like invisible threads pulling tighter with each truth she uncovered.

Her last stop brought her to Harriet.

The event coordinator was standing near the produce stands with a stack of paperwork held tight to her chest. She looked tired, her usual pin neat hairstyle losing its grip on a few strands.

"Harriet?" Mara said softly.

Harriet turned.

"Ah," Harriet said. "Mara. I was hoping to see you. I have something to discuss."

Her tone was sharper than usual, clipped and cool.

"What is wrong?" Mara asked.

"Funding," Harriet said curtly. "For the upcoming winter festival."

Mara blinked. "Funding?"

"Yes," Harriet said. "Owen donated a significant amount each year. It was always part of the planning process. With him gone, certain committees will have to reorganize. And some people are already whispering about who may have influenced yesterday's events."

Mara felt her breath hitch. "Are you implying I had anything to do with—"

"I am implying nothing," Harriet said quickly. "But people talk. They always talk. Especially when tragedy affects community finances."

Mara stared at her, stunned.

"Harriet," she said quietly, "I lost my snowglobe. I watched someone collapse in front of me. My bakery is in trouble. I am the last person who wants this."

Harriet's stern expression wavered.

"I know," she murmured. "I am sorry. I am overwhelmed. This entire situation disrupts everything, and I need answers before the town grows more divided."

Mara swallowed.

"Did you see anything that might help?" she asked.

Harriet paused.

"I saw Owen meet someone before the brunch started," Harriet said slowly. "Near the side hallway. Their conversation looked tense. I planned to ask him about it later. Now I cannot."

"Did you recognize the other person?" Mara asked.

"No," Harriet said softly. "Only the coat. Dark wool. Black buttons on the cuffs."

Mara's breath caught.

The same coat from Jenna's photo.

The same kind of glove.

The same shadowy figure.

Harriet rubbed her temples. "I should not even be talking about this. But someone has to say something real instead of gossip."

Mara nodded.

"Thank you for telling me," she said.

Harriet sighed. "Just be careful. Do not draw attention to yourself. Not right now."

Mara left the market with her coat pulled tight, the cold air biting at her cheeks.

Tessa's land.

Mark's eviction threats.

Harriet's funding panic.

The envelope.

The snowglobe.

The shadowy figure in the hallway.

Motives tugged at the edges of every conversation she had.

She descended the steps of the Old Mill Market feeling like the ground beneath her was no longer as steady as it had been a week ago. Frostberry Hollow was a small town, but secrets lived in its corners just as thickly as snow drifted across its rooftops.

One thing became painfully clear.

Everyone connected to Owen had something to hide.

And someone among them had far more to lose than the rest.

Chapter 9

By late afternoon the clouds had settled low over Frostberry Hollow, dimming the daylight into something that looked more like early evening. The snow that had drifted gently all morning thickened into a steady fall, soft flakes teaming up to blur the outlines of rooftops and lamp posts.

Mara stood at the front window of the bakery and watched it for a moment, her reflection overlapping the view outside. Her eyes looked tired in the glass. Thin lines of worry gathered at the corners.

On the street, a few bundled figures hurried past with their heads down. Across the way, Daniel Royce's antiques shop glowed softly, its front window crowded with lamps, clocks, and the sort of curiosities that invited long, curious looks. The sign above the door, Royce & Relics, swayed gently in the winter wind.

She remembered the photos Jenna had shown her, the gloved hand, the dark sleeve. Harriet's offhand comment about the buttons. Tessa's story about the well. Mark's frustration. All of it swirled together like the flakes outside, refusing to settle into a clear picture.

She had one name remaining on her mental list for the day.

Daniel.

"You are staring hard enough to melt the snow," Jenna said softly from behind her.

Mara turned. Jenna sat at a table with her laptop open, editing the brunch photos again, pausing often to frown at the screen.

"Just thinking," Mara said. "I need to talk to him."

"Daniel?" Jenna asked.

"Yes."

"Want backup?" Jenna closed the laptop halfway.

Mara hesitated.

"Stay here with Ellie," she said. "In case customers actually come in. Or in case Connor drops by again. I will not be long."

Ellie, who sat on a stool behind the counter wrapping cookie samples, raised an eyebrow.

"You mean you are going to walk into the shop of a man who knows all the town's secrets, sells mysterious antiques, and has a calm smile that could mean anything," Ellie said. "Alone."

"That sounds dramatic," Mara said.

"It is accurate," Ellie replied.

Jenna shrugged. "At least let us know if you plan to do anything more dangerous than ask questions."

"Questions only," Mara said. "I promise."

She grabbed her coat and scarf, wrapped them tightly around herself, and stepped out into the cold.

The winter air bit at her cheeks. Snowflakes collected on her eyelashes, melting into tiny, cold drops. She crossed the street carefully, boots crunching over a thin layer of packed snow.

A brass bell chimed softly when she pushed open the antiques shop door.

The air inside smelled of dust, lemon oil, and something faintly metallic. Lamps of all styles and ages glowed softly from tables and shelves, casting pockets of warm light across rows of items. Brass compasses, old cameras, stacks of faded books with soft leather covers, twisted glass bottles that looked like they had once held secrets.

Daniel stood behind a glass counter, sorting through a box of tarnished silver spoons. He looked up at once when he heard the bell.

"Mara," he said, his face brightening. "You picked a good time. The shop is quiet. Everyone else is hiding from the snow."

"That might have been my plan too," she said. "Your shop always looks warmer from across the street."

"It is warmer," he said. "That is because I bribe the radiators."

She smiled despite herself.

"Do you have a moment?" she asked.

"For you, sure," he said. "Everything all right?"

She stepped closer, unwinding her scarf. "Not exactly."

His eyes grew more serious at once.

"Sit," he said, gesturing to a cushioned chair near the counter. "You look like you have been arguing with ghosts."

"That is not far from the truth," she said softly.

She sat. He leaned against the counter, close enough to listen but not so close as to crowd her.

"The bakery?" he asked. "The whispers?"

"Yes," she said. "And something else."

She described the photos Jenna had shown her. The envelope. The gloved hand. The dark wool sleeve. Harriet's mention of the same coat near the side hallway. His expression grew more thoughtful with each detail.

"Let me guess," he said quietly. "You are trying to figure out who the mystery person is."

"Yes," she said. "Do you have any idea?"

Daniel rubbed the bridge of his nose.

"Half the town shops here," he said. "I see a lot of coats and gloves. But that combination sounds familiar."

"Familiar how?" she pressed.

"Those gloves," he said. "Lined leather with a small black button. I sold a pair like that last month. Only one pair in that exact style."

"Who bought them?" she asked.

Daniel hesitated.

"Do you know what you are asking me to do?" he said gently. "Sharing customer purchases is not exactly good for business."

"I know," she said. "But someone met Owen in secret. Someone gave him an envelope shortly before he died. Someone was near the hallway and could have taken my snowglobe. This is not about curiosity anymore."

His gaze searched hers.

"Connor is handling the official investigation," he said. "Have you talked to him about the photos?"

"Not yet," Mara admitted. "I wanted to see what I could find first. And I did not want to hand him something half understood."

"You do not trust him?" Daniel asked.

"I do," she said. "But I also know he is overwhelmed. And I am the one whose bakery is under a shadow. I cannot sit still and wait. I need to understand what is happening around me."

Daniel studied her for a long moment, then sighed.

"Stay here," he said.

He went into the back room, leaving her alone with the soft ticking of several clocks and the distant sound of wind brushing against the windows.

Mara glanced around the shop. She noticed a shelf lined with small wooden boxes, each bound with thin metal clasps. A row of pocket watches. A heavy mirror with a frame carved into curling leaves.

On a lower shelf, a few snowglobes sat in a neat row.

Her breath caught.

She slid to the edge of her chair and leaned closer.

These were older than her aunt's designs. Dust clung lightly to the glass. One held a miniature train station. Another showed a lighthouse, its painted light fading. The third was a simple house beneath a tree.

She wondered how many hands had shaken them, how many people had watched the tiny storms swirl and settle.

She reached for the lighthouse globe, then pulled her hand back, uncertain if she should touch anything without Daniel nearby.

Footsteps sounded.

Daniel returned with a small leather notebook in one hand. The edges were worn and soft, pages stuffed with scraps of paper where he had added notes.

"This is my sales log," he said. "Handwritten. Old fashioned. I never trusted computers fully."

"Probably wise," she said.

He opened the notebook and flipped through several pages, scanning quickly.

"Gloves," he murmured. "Black button. Lined leather. Here."

He tapped a line and squinted.

"Purchased by Harriet Dove," he said.

Mara blinked.

"Harriet?" she repeated. "The same Harriet who organizes every event and worries about funding?"

"The very one," Daniel said.

Mara's mind raced. She pictured Harriet standing near the auction table, clipboard in hand. Harriet moving through the hall before the brunch, adjusting decorations. Harriet mentioning seeing Owen near the hallway herself.

"Are you sure?" Mara asked.

Daniel gave her a wry look.

"I know my own handwriting," he said. "And Harriet is one of my most loyal customers. She spends half her disposable income on antique lamps and decorative boxes. She wanted gloves that matched a particular coat."

"The dark wool coat," Mara whispered.

He nodded.

"She said she did not see the other person's face," Mara said. "She told me that. Maybe she left something out."

"Maybe," Daniel said. "Or maybe someone borrowed her coat and gloves. Or maybe there is more than one pair in town and I am being unfair."

His tone was cautious. He was careful not to leap to conclusions.

Mara wished she could do the same.

"Did you sell any miniatures like the lantern in my snowglobe?" she asked.

Daniel nodded slowly.

"Yes," he said. "Actually, that is why I was not surprised when you came in. I had a feeling this might be coming."

He set the notebook down and walked to a glass case. From inside, he took a small padded tray that held tiny metal figures used in doll houses and decorative projects. He plucked one small piece from the corner and brought it back.

It was nearly identical to the one in her snowglobe. A miniature lamp post, no higher than her thumb.

"I sold one of these to Owen the day before the brunch," Daniel said. "He said he needed a specific size and style. He had the measurements handwritten on a scrap of paper."

"Did he say why?" she asked.

"No," Daniel said. "And I did not ask. It is my job to supply odd little treasures, not interrogate customers."

"But you remember it," she said.

"How could I forget?" he said. "He was particular about the details. That always sticks in my mind."

"And you did not mention this to Connor?" she asked.

"Not yet," Daniel said. "He has not asked. I figured he had enough on his plate without me telling him Owen had a sudden interest in doll sized lamps."

Mara's thoughts spun.

Owen had bought a miniature lamp. She had made a snowglobe featuring a lamp at the center of a bridge. Someone had stolen that snowglobe. Someone wearing gloves that might be connected to Harriet.

"Do you think Owen came to you because of my snowglobes?" she asked.

"Possibly," Daniel said. "He asked if I knew much about them."

"What did you tell him?"

"I told him Iris was the expert," Daniel said. "And that you had taken over. He asked if they were easy to tamper with."

Mara's stomach dropped.

"To tamper with?" she repeated.

"Yes," Daniel said slowly. "He wanted to know if someone could add something inside the base. A compartment. Or if that was impossible once the pieces were set."

Mara heard her pulse pounding in her ears.

"What did you say?" she managed.

"I told him it was possible," Daniel said, face grave. "Difficult. But possible. He asked what kind of tools he might need. I said he would be better off talking to you. He did not like that answer."

"So he tried to learn how to hide something in a snowglobe," she murmured. "And someone else decided to take mine."

The thought made her dizzy.

"Connor needs to know this," she said.

"I agree," Daniel said. "If there is any connection between the snowglobe and his death, it might start here."

"Will you tell him?" she asked.

"I will," Daniel said. "I will call him after you leave. Hearing it from a shop owner may carry more weight than secondhand knowledge."

Relief washed through her, brief but real.

"Thank you," she said. "For trusting me with this."

"Trust goes both ways," he said. "You trusted me with your worry. I trust you to handle this carefully. Do not go chasing suspects yourself, all right?"

Mara tried to smile.

"We both know I am not built for chasing," she said. "I trip on flat floors."

He chuckled gently. "Fair point."

The bell over the door chimed again.

They both turned.

A customer stepped inside, shaking snow from their coat. Mara recognized the figure at once.

Harriet Dove.

Her coat was dark wool. Her gloves were lined leather with small black buttons at the wrist.

"Of course," Jenna had once said, "Harriet is married to schedules and style."

Now the style looked different to Mara. It looked like a puzzle piece.

Harriet stopped short when she saw them together. Her gaze flicked from Daniel to Mara and back again.

"Oh," she said stiffly. "I did not realize you had company. I can come back later."

"Stay," Daniel said smoothly. "We were just finishing. Mara was checking on a potential display item for the bakery."

It was a small lie, but a kind one.

Harriet's shoulders relaxed slightly.

Mara forced her voice to stay steady.

"I should head back to the bakery," she said. "We have a few afternoon orders."

"Of course," Harriet said. "I hope business picks up."

Mara could not tell if the words were sincere or polite.

She threaded her scarf around her neck again and moved toward the door. As she passed Harriet, she could not help but glance at the gloves. The stitches. The buttons. The way the dark wool sleeve overlapped the cuffs.

She remembered the photo. The hand. The envelope.

She stepped out into the cold, her mind buzzing.

Behind her, soft voices drifted faintly through the door for a moment before it closed fully. She could not make out the words.

The street felt emptier now, as if the town itself were holding its breath.

Mara crossed back to the bakery, each step heavy with the knowledge she carried.

Owen had bought a miniature lamp.

Owen had probed Daniel about secret compartments.

Someone with gloves like Harriet's had given Owen an envelope and lurked near the hallway.

Someone had stolen her snowglobe.

The suspects were no longer distant names and faces. They were neighbors. Colleagues. Friends.

She paused outside the bakery door, hand resting on the handle.

Inside, the air would be warm. The ovens would hum. Ellie and Jenna would ask what she had learned.

Outside, the snow continued to fall, muffling the sounds of the town and tucking secrets under its soft white cover.

Mara pulled the door open and stepped inside, carrying those secrets with her, knowing this was only the beginning of what she would uncover.

Chapter 10

Evening settled over Frostberry Hollow with a quiet weight, the kind that made the snow covered rooftops look almost sleepy under the pale glow of the streetlights. The town had already begun to drift into nighttime stillness as Mara walked toward the bakery, her boots crunching softly over the thin frost that had formed on the sidewalks.

She had stayed late with Ellie and Jenna, walking them most of the way home before turning back on her own. They had offered to accompany her, but she had insisted she would be fine. She needed a few minutes of quiet to sort her thoughts.

The bakery's windows glowed gently, warming the color of the snow piled against the building. Mara paused before unlocking the door, feeling a tug of gratitude. No matter what storm brewed around her, the Cozy Nook Bakery always looked like a small safe haven in the winter nights.

She slipped the key into the lock, turned it, and stepped inside.

The silence felt heavier than she expected. Usually the building hummed with the faint clicks and creaks of cooling ovens and settling wood. Tonight, something was different. Still. Almost expectant.

She closed the door behind her and turned on one of the hanging lights.

The main counter looked normal. Chairs neatly tucked in. Display case empty but clean. The lingering scent of cinnamon, flour and baked sugar held fast in the air. Everything seemed untouched.

Mara exhaled.

Maybe she was just tired.

She carried her bag to the counter, set her gloves beside it, and headed toward the back hallway to grab a ledger she had forgotten earlier.

Halfway there, she stopped.

The hallway light was already on.

She had turned it off when they left.

A small chill crept up her spine.

"Hello?" she called softly.

Her voice sounded too loud in the stillness.

No answer.

She stepped forward slowly and peered into the supply room.

Her breath caught.

The shelves looked wrong. Not chaotic, but shifted. Moved. As if someone had run their hands across every item, checking, comparing, examining.

Boxes of miniatures that she used for her snowglobes were pulled forward from their usual positions. One small container lay open on its side, its tiny metal pieces scattered in the shape of a spill that had not been cleaned. Her extra tools sat out of order. The paint brushes were no longer lined up in their cup. The jar of varnish was uncapped, sitting precariously near the edge of the table.

Nothing looked destroyed. Nothing smashed. But everything had been touched.

Her pulse beat hard in her throat.

She stepped into the room slowly.

The wooden floor creaked under her foot, making her flinch.

She scanned the space again, her eyes trying to stitch detail into sense.

Someone had gone through her miniatures.

Someone had studied her tools.

Someone had searched her creations.

The thought came with a cold certainty.

They were looking for something.

Her hands shook slightly as she crouched to pick up a tiny metal tree that had rolled under her worktable. She placed it back in the container, though her eyes never left the doorway.

What had they been trying to find?

One of her aunt's old pieces?

A miniature that looked like the one inside the stolen snowglobe?

A spare lamp?

Another compartment she did not know existed?

Her breath hitched at the thought.

She stepped back into the hall, pulled out her phone with trembling fingers, and scrolled to Ellie's number.

Before she could press call, the front door opened with a soft jingle.

Mara startled so hard she almost dropped her phone.

"Mara?" Ellie's voice called. "Are you still here?"

Mara sagged against the wall with relief.

"In the back," she managed.

Ellie hurried over, coat half buttoned, breath forming small clouds.

"I realized you left your scarf at the corner café," Ellie said. "I wanted to bring it back before you froze tomorrow morning. I did not mean to scare you."

Mara swallowed and pointed toward the supply room.

"I found something," she said.

Ellie followed her inside.

For a long moment Ellie did not speak. She scanned the shelves, the shifted boxes, the open container.

"Someone was in here," Ellie said quietly.

"Yes," Mara whispered.

Ellie bent down, lifted a miniature bridge that had been separated from its set, and placed it carefully back into the box.

"They were looking for something," Ellie said. "Not stealing. Searching."

Mara nodded. "But what?"

Ellie looked at her with a gentleness that made tears prick at the corners of Mara's eyes.

"Something connected to the snowglobe," Ellie said. "It has to be. Either they wanted to know how your aunt made them or they were trying to see if you had another one like the missing globe."

"But they did not take anything," Mara said. "Not even the rare miniatures. Those are expensive. Collectors hunt for them."

"That tells us something important," Ellie said, straightening. "This was not a robbery. This was deliberate."

The room seemed colder now, despite the warmth from the nearby oven.

Mara rubbed her arms.

"I cannot stay here tonight," she whispered.

"You should not," Ellie agreed. "Come home with me or with Jenna."

Mara shook her head. "I will stay at my place. But I will not sleep much."

Ellie stepped closer and rested her hands gently on Mara's shoulders.

"You are not alone," Ellie said. "Not in this. Not for a moment. But you need to call Connor in the morning. This break in matters. It is a clue."

Mara nodded.

Ellie glanced at the door.

"We will also need stronger locks," Ellie said. "And maybe a camera. Something discreet. Whoever did this might come back."

Mara felt the weight of the truth settle on her like snow gathering on windowsills.

She stepped back into the hallway, staring at the room she had always associated with creation and warmth. Now it felt unfamiliar. A place someone had trespassed, rifling through the pieces of her craft, her memories, her connection to Iris.

Ellie touched her arm again.

"Let us go," she said softly. "You should not be here alone tonight."

Mara nodded, grabbed her coat and bag, and followed Ellie out.

As she locked the bakery door behind her, she glanced once more through the window.

Everything inside looked quiet and still.

But Mara no longer trusted the quiet.

She tugged her coat tighter and walked into the snowy night, aware now that the mystery surrounding her had reached inside her walls, touching her life in a way she could no longer ignore.

She would protect the bakery.

She would protect her aunt's craft.

And she would find the truth behind the shadows creeping into Frostberry Hollow.

One way or another.

Chapter 11

Morning settled slowly over Frostberry Hollow, leaving pale streaks of soft gold across rooftops and a fresh dusting of powdery snow at every doorstep. The world looked deceptively peaceful, wrapped in a quiet that made the night's unease feel even sharper in Mara's chest.

She arrived at the bakery earlier than usual, wanting the comforting routine of morning prep to settle her pulse. The bell above the door chimed softly as she entered, the warm air greeting her with familiar scents. Cinnamon. Cooling flour. A faint trace of vanilla that seemed woven into the walls after years of baking.

For a moment, Mara allowed herself to simply breathe.

But when she moved toward the back hallway, the memory of last night's discovery rushed back in vivid detail. The supply room shelves shifted. The open box of miniatures. The tools moved. Someone had not only entered her bakery, but searched through pieces of herself.

She stepped inside the supply room again, just to prove to herself it was real.

It was.

In the morning light, the disruption appeared even clearer. Each miniature slightly off center. Boxes not aligned. A subtle tidiness, yet so wrong that her skin prickled.

She touched the edge of the worktable and closed her eyes.

"Not today," she whispered. "I will not start today with fear."

Footsteps sounded in the main bakery. The bell had not chimed, which meant someone had opened the door quietly, or with a key. Mara tensed instinctively.

"Mara?" a familiar voice called.

She stepped into the hallway.

Connor Hale stood near the counter, snow still melting on the shoulders of his uniform jacket. His expression was serious, but not unkind. The kind of seriousness that meant something important was coming.

"Sheriff," Mara said softly. "You startled me."

"I tried knocking," Connor said. "You must not have heard."

"No," she said. "I was in the back."

He studied her face a moment longer than necessary.

"You look tired," he said.

"I am," she admitted. "And you look like you have news I will not enjoy hearing."

Connor's jaw tightened slightly.

"I do have news," he said. "But let us sit. This is not something to rush through while you stand there shaking."

Mara blinked. "I am not shaking."

Connor gave her a look that said otherwise.

They both sat at one of the corner tables. The bakery still felt quiet, too early for customers. The snow outside muffled the town, making the moment feel fragile.

Connor rested his hat on the table and folded his hands.

"I should start by saying you are not in trouble," he said.

Her breath loosened a little.

"But we made a discovery during our search of Owen Barrow's possessions," he continued. "Something unexpected."

Mara felt her pulse rise. "What sort of discovery?"

Connor reached into his coat and placed a folder on the table. She recognized the smooth, official cardstock of sheriff's office files. He did not open it yet.

"Do you remember telling me your snowglobe was taken at the brunch?" he asked.

"Of course I do," Mara said. "It vanished right after Owen collapsed. I assumed someone stole it to hide something inside."

"Well," Connor said slowly, "the snowglobe has turned up."

Mara's breath hitched.

"Where?" she asked, leaning forward. "Where did you find it?"

Connor opened the folder and slid a photograph across the table. It showed a plain black briefcase, scuffed at the edges, resting on a forensic paper sheet. The briefcase was unlatched and open.

Inside sat her snowglobe. Her exact snowglobe.

Mara pressed a hand to her mouth.

"He had it?" she whispered.

"Yes," Connor said. "Owen Barrow was carrying your snowglobe inside his briefcase when he died."

She stared at the photograph, her mind spinning.

"But... it was on the auction table," she said. "I placed it there. People saw it. Harriet saw it. It was right there."

"We have reason to believe Owen removed it before the collapse," Connor said. "Possibly during the hour when people were taking their seats for the brunch."

Mara shook her head slowly. "I never saw him near the table."

"He may have waited for a moment when your back was turned," Connor said. "Or he may have used the crowd for cover. Plenty of people were milling around."

Mara felt dizzy with questions.

"Why would he take it?" she whispered.

"That is the part that concerns me," Connor said. "Because when we found it, the snowglobe was not exactly as you created it."

Mara felt a cold shiver slide down her spine. She looked at Connor, barely breathing.

"What do you mean?" she asked.

Connor turned the folder around and opened it fully.

Inside were close up photos of the snowglobe. The glass sphere. The snowy miniature creek. The tiny bridge. The lamp at the center.

Except something was wrong.

Where the miniature lamp should have stood, there was a small hollow gap in the base. A carved pocket where the lamp had been removed.

In its place lay a tightly rolled scrap of paper.

Her heart pounded like a drum in her ribs.

"No," she whispered. "That lamp was secured. It should not come out without loosening several pieces. It should not… it cannot…"

"It came out," Connor said gently. "And someone put that paper inside."

Mara pressed a trembling hand against the table.

"Did Owen hide it there?" she asked.

"That is one possibility," Connor said. "But it could also mean someone else did, and Owen discovered it."

Mara stared at the pictures.

Her beautiful snowglobe. The careful detail she had painted. The tiny world she had crafted with such love.

Now dissected. Altered. Turned into a container for something secret.

Her stomach twisted at the thought.

"What is written on the paper?" she asked.

Connor hesitated.

"We are still analyzing it," he said. "But I can tell you the note was not a simple message. It may be part of a larger set of information."

"Part of a set?" Mara echoed. "Like... a clue?"

"Possibly," Connor said. "And it concerns Owen's business dealings."

Mara swallowed hard.

"What did it say?" she pressed.

Connor shook his head slowly.

"You know I cannot reveal all the details yet," he said. "Part of this becomes evidence in a larger case. But I can give you one piece to prepare you."

She leaned forward, bracing herself.

"The rolled paper mentions land," Connor said quietly. "It refers to properties in Frostberry Hollow. Deeds. Transactions. And something that no one has been able to trace yet."

Mara felt her breath leave in a rush.

Land deeds.

Tessa's stories about Owen pushing for her property.

Mark's struggle with the eviction attempts.

Harriet's funding fears tangled with town development.

The well on Tessa's land.

The envelope in the photo.

It clicked in a way that made her chest tighten.

"Someone used my snowglobe," she whispered. "Used it as a hiding place for a clue about land. Why would they choose my piece?"

"Because your snowglobes are finely crafted," Connor said. "Detailed. And the bases are heavier than they appear. Someone with experience knew they could carve out space without drawing attention."

Mara stared at him.

"You think my aunt may have known something?" she asked.

Connor hesitated again. "I think Iris Linden knew many things. People trusted her. They confided in her. She helped half this town keep their secrets safe. It is possible she had knowledge she did not share widely."

Mara felt a swirl of emotion. Pride. Loss. Confusion. Fear.

"What does this mean?" she asked.

"It means the snowglobe is not just sentimental," Connor said. "It was chosen because it was important. And you inherited something that may be bigger than you realize."

Mara stared at the photograph again. At the hollow space

where her miniature lamp had once stood. At the rolled scrap of paper that had rested inside.

Her hands trembled.

Connor leaned closer, lowering his voice.

"I also need to warn you," he said. "If the snowglobe was used to transport hidden information, then someone knew it was valuable. Someone knew where to look. Which means the break in at your bakery was not random."

Her eyes widened.

"Someone thinks there is more," she whispered.

Connor nodded once. "Yes."

A shiver raced through Mara's body at the thought.

She wrapped her arms around herself, cold despite the heat from the bakery ovens.

"I did not ask for any of this," she whispered. "I just wanted to bake. And make snowglobes. And have a quiet life."

"I know," Connor said softly. "But sometimes trouble finds good people because someone else made bad choices."

She let those words settle heavily in the room.

"What should I do?" she asked.

Connor looked at her with a seriousness that made her chest ache.

"You stay alert," he said. "You lock your doors. You call me if anything feels off. And you let me know if you remember anything about the globe. Anything at all."

Mara nodded.

Connor gathered his folder, stood, and placed his hat back on.

"I will return once the lab finishes analyzing the paper," he said. "If there is more hidden in your aunt's work, we will find it."

He walked toward the door, paused, and looked back.

"Do not carry all of this alone," he said gently.

Then he stepped out into the snow.

Mara stood by the table for a long time, staring at the photograph.

Her snowglobe had come back.

But it carried secrets she had never imagined.

Secrets that pointed to land deeds... and someone willing to hide them in her work.

She pressed a trembling hand to her heart.

"This is only the beginning," she whispered.

And she knew she was right.

The bakery remained quiet long after Connor left, a hush that settled over the room with a heaviness that made it hard for Mara to breathe. Snow drifted steadily outside the window, blurring the shapes of the streetlights and washing the morning in muted gray.

She stood at the table staring at the photograph of the snowglobe as if it might tell her something new. But all she could see was the hollow space where her miniature lantern had once stood. Empty. Violated. Repurposed for something secret.

A knock at the bakery door startled her.

Mara flinched but forced herself to breathe slowly. She approached the door and pulled it open.

Ellie stood on the steps bundled in a thick brown coat and holding a thermos. Snowflakes clung to her hair and scarf.

"I brought hot chocolate," Ellie announced gently. "You sounded strange on the phone earlier."

"I am sorry," Mara whispered. "I did not mean to sound upset."

"You did," Ellie said, stepping inside. "And that is all right. You have every reason to be upset."

She closed the door behind her, stamped snow from her boots, and followed Mara to the corner table. When she saw the photographs, she inhaled sharply.

"Oh," she said softly. "It really was found."

Mara nodded. Her throat felt thick. "In Owen's briefcase."

Ellie lowered herself into a chair with slow caution, as though one wrong movement might unsettle everything in the room.

"Show me," she said.

Mara slid the pictures toward her. Ellie studied them one by one, eyes sharpening.

"They pulled the lantern out," Ellie whispered. "Someone had to use a thin tool to pry it loose."

"I know," Mara said softly.

Ellie shook her head with a mixture of anger and disbelief.

"Whoever did this must have known what they were doing," Ellie said. "This is not something a random thief could manage."

Mara rubbed her hands together. "Connor said someone might have known my aunt's work. Knew what could be hidden in the base."

Ellie's face softened with sympathy. "Oh, Mara."

"I do not know what to believe," Mara admitted. "I feel like every assumption I had about this town is becoming tangled."

"Well," Ellie said, pouring hot chocolate into two cups, "that just means we untangle it one knot at a time."

Mara managed a weak smile.

A few moments later the bell above the door chimed again. Jenna barreled in with her laptop bag over one shoulder, cheeks flushed from the cold.

"Tell me everything right now," Jenna said breathlessly. "Ellie called. I had barely finished brushing my teeth."

Mara blinked. "Ellie called you?"

"I was not sure if you wanted to talk," Ellie said gently. "And the last thing you need is to sit alone with this."

Mara squeezed Ellie's hand. "Thank you."

Jenna placed her laptop on the table and leaned over the photographs.

"Oh wow," Jenna whispered. "They really found it."

"In Owen's briefcase," Mara said.

Jenna stared at her, stunned. "So he really did take it. He must have known something was inside."

"Yes," Mara said. "And whoever hid the rolled paper must have believed the snowglobe was the safest place."

"But why leave it there?" Jenna asked. "Why hide a clue about land deeds inside a snowglobe that would be auctioned to the public? Anyone could have ended up with it."

Ellie shook her head.

"Maybe the plan was for Owen to win it at the auction," Ellie said. "He could have bid on it easily. He had the money. Maybe the person who hid the clue assumed he would ensure he got it."

Mara frowned. "That still does not explain why the clue was inside mine. There were other items. Other places to hide things."

Ellie looked at her with a gentle expression.

"Your aunt made snowglobes for decades," Ellie said. "People trusted her work. She might have made one for someone in the past with this exact purpose."

"But the miniature lantern," Mara whispered. "Why that detail?"

Jenna opened her laptop and pulled up the brunch photos again.

"Let me look at the earlier shots," Jenna said. "Maybe I captured something about the snowglobe table. Or the briefcase. Or the people who stood near it."

She clicked through image after image. The buffer of faces and laughter no longer felt warm to Mara. It felt eerie. Each photo a piece of proof from a moment she had not fully understood.

Jenna paused at a picture of the auction table.

The snowglobe gleamed at the center of the frame. Bright. Beautiful. Innocent.

"You took this maybe twenty minutes before the collapse," Mara whispered.

"Yes," Jenna said. "And look. Nothing about it seems disturbed. The lamp is clearly in place."

Ellie leaned over. "Which means someone removed it after this moment but before Owen collapsed."

Jenna flipped forward.

A photo showed Owen standing near a group of local officials, the tension in his posture clear even in the still image.

"And he had his briefcase with him," Jenna murmured. "I remember thinking it looked odd for a brunch."

Ellie straightened slowly. "It makes sense now. He intended to hide or retrieve something."

Mara's pulse quickened.

"Connor said the rolled paper mentioned land," she whispered. "Land deeds. Transactions. Something hidden."

Jenna looked up sharply. "Land like Tessa's? The well?"

"Land like Mark's store," Ellie added. "Or the houses Owen wanted to buy for development."

"Or the festival land Harriet needed funding for," Jenna said. "She said she was desperate."

Mara swallowed.

"Everyone who argued with Owen," she whispered. "Everyone who had something to gain or lose... all of them have ties to land."

Jenna paused the photo slideshow.

"Mara," Jenna said softly, "I think you need to tell us what is on that paper."

"I do not know more than what Connor told me," Mara said. "Only that the clue concerns land deeds."

Ellie leaned back in her chair, thinking.

"You know what this means," Ellie said slowly. "This was not random. Someone hid that clue for a reason. Either to expose something Owen was doing... or to keep that information out of someone else's hands."

"And Owen knew it," Mara whispered. "Otherwise he would not have taken the snowglobe."

Jenna nodded. "He wanted whatever was inside. And someone else wanted it too."

Ellie clasped her hands.

"This brings us to a new problem," she said. "If someone already broke into your bakery looking for more clues… they may believe you still have something connected to the snowglobe."

Mara's heart thudded hard.

She looked at her shelves of miniatures. Her snowglobe designs. The tools that had belonged to her aunt.

"What could they be hoping to find here?" she whispered.

"Another hidden compartment," Ellie said. "Or another piece your aunt never told anyone about. Something they think you might know without realizing it."

Mara pressed her hands to her temples.

"This is too much," she admitted. "I just want the bakery to survive. Now I am caught in the middle of land deals and secrets I do not understand."

Ellie reached out and squeezed her arm.

"You will not face this alone," Ellie said. "We will figure this out. Together."

Jenna nodded firmly.

"And we will start by figuring out what the clue means," Jenna said. "We know the paper mentioned land deeds. Which implies records. Transfers. Maybe fraud."

Mara felt a tremor of recognition.

"My aunt," she whispered. "She mentioned something to me once. A strange conversation she overheard years ago. Something about old land rights and a disagreement between two families."

Ellie straightened in her chair. "When did she tell you this?"

"Years ago," Mara said. "I did not think anything of it. She did not give details. Just said this town had older stories than people liked to admit."

"And maybe someone wanted one of those old stories to stay buried," Jenna said quietly.

Mara stared at her hands.

Everything felt like a puzzle made of snowflakes. Fragile. Cold. And falling apart faster than she could catch.

Her phone buzzed on the table.

The screen lit with a name.

Harriet Dove.

Ellie and Jenna exchanged glances.

"Do you want to answer?" Jenna asked.

Mara swallowed hard.

She pressed accept.

"Hello?" she said.

"Mara," Harriet said. Her voice sounded strained, tighter than usual. "I heard Connor visited you. I wanted to check on you."

Mara forced her voice steady. "I am managing."

"Good," Harriet said. "Listen. I may need to speak with you privately this afternoon about something important. Something connected to the brunch."

Mara hesitated.

"What sort of something?" she asked.

There was a long pause.

"It concerns Owen's business files," Harriet said finally. "And something he asked me to sign last week."

Mara glanced at Ellie and Jenna, who leaned in closer.

"Are you safe to talk?" Mara asked softly.

Harriet's breath caught. "Not on the phone."

"Come by the bakery," Mara said.

"No," Harriet whispered. "I will meet you at the library. Half an hour."

The line clicked off.

Mara slowly lowered the phone.

"What was that?" Ellie asked.

"She knows something," Mara whispered. "Something about Owen. Something about the land."

Jenna folded her arms. "Do you want us to come with you?"

Mara nodded.

"Yes," she said softly. "I am done doing this alone."

Outside, the snowfall thickened into a quiet veil.

Inside, Mara, Ellie and Jenna gathered their things, unaware that Harriet's revelation would become the spark that finally illuminated the truth behind the snowglobe's secret.

* * *

The walk to the Frostberry Hollow Library felt longer than usual, though the building stood only a few blocks from the bakery. Snow drifted steadily in soft waves that seemed to swallow sound, muting the town beneath its shifting veil. Mara walked between Ellie and Jenna, their boots crunching in unison over the fresh powder.

The library's tall brick façade emerged from the white haze, its old stone steps swept clean, its lamps glowing like warm beacons in the winter gloom. Mara took a slow breath and pushed the door open.

Inside, warmth greeted them instantly. The scent of polished wood, well loved books, and a faint hint of pine cleaner filled the entrance. Tall shelves stood in neat rows under the soft glow of iron framed lamps. The library always had a certain reverent stillness, like a place that protected not only stories but also confessions.

Harriet waited in one of the far reading nooks, sitting stiffly in a cushioned armchair. Her coat was draped neatly over the next seat, her gloves folded on top. Her posture was straight, her hands clasped with the tension of someone holding herself together only by habit.

When she saw Mara approach, she stood.

"You came," Harriet said.

"We did," Mara replied.

Harriet hesitated at the sight of Ellie and Jenna.

"I thought you would come alone," Harriet murmured. "This may not be easy to hear."

"We are all in this now," Ellie said gently. "You do not have to speak to us alone."

Harriet pressed a hand to her forehead, as if trying to push away a headache.

"Very well," she said, sinking back into her chair. "Sit. All of you."

The three women settled on the bench across from her. Mara's heart thudded with a quiet rhythm she felt in her fingers, in her ribs, in her thoughts.

Harriet looked down at her hands for a long moment before speaking.

"What I am about to tell you," she began softly, "was not meant to leave my desk. I never intended to be part of Owen's dealings. But he left me no choice."

Mara leaned forward.

"What dealings?" Mara asked.

Harriet swallowed.

"A week before the brunch," Harriet said, "Owen brought me a set of documents. Contracts. Agreements for future land acquisitions tied to his development plans. He claimed the town council needed a signature from a community liaison to move forward."

Ellie stiffened. "But you are not a liaison. You are an event coordinator."

"Yes," Harriet said, voice strained. "Which is exactly why he chose me. He said the council wanted someone neutral. Someone not tied to business. Someone who already had the trust of the town."

Jenna frowned. "But that does not make sense. You would need authority to sign for the town."

"I told him that," Harriet said. "Repeatedly. But he insisted the paperwork was already approved. He said all I needed to do was sign on behalf of the festival committee for grant purposes."

Mara's stomach twisted.

"Harriet," she whispered. "Did you sign?"

Harriet lifted her gaze, eyes glossy with regret.

"No," Harriet said. "I refused. Something felt wrong. The numbers did not add up. And the properties listed... they were not festival properties."

"Which properties?" Mara asked quietly.

Harriet looked at her without blinking.

"Tessa's land," Harriet said. "Mark's store building. An old parcel near the creek that has been unclaimed for years. And one of the hillside plots the town protects as a natural reserve."

Mara felt her chest tighten.

"All of them?" she whispered.

Harriet nodded.

"Owen told me he was consolidating land to prepare for a large winter resort project. He claimed it would bring money and visitors. But the more he spoke, the more I realized this had nothing to do with community benefit. He was preparing for something... hidden."

Jenna leaned forward. "Something like old land rights? Underground tunnels? The well on Tessa's land?"

Harriet stiffened. "He mentioned the well. He said it connected to older property records. He said the festival land traced back to deeds that were never properly transferred in the early days of the town."

Mara exchanged a glance with Ellie.

Land deeds.

The clue in the snowglobe.

The miniature lantern hidden in the base.

Owen's private meeting with the gloved figure.

All of it rattled inside her mind, forming a shape she still could not fully see.

"There is more," Harriet said.

Mara breathed in.

"Tell us."

Harriet reached into her purse with trembling fingers and pulled out a folded sheet of paper. Not a photograph. Not a letter. A photocopy.

"This came to my mailbox yesterday," Harriet said. "No return address."

She handed it to Mara.

Mara unfolded it.

Her breath caught.

It was a photocopy of a land deed.

Old. Yellowed originally, though the copy muted the age.

The top corner bore a faint stamp from the early days of Frostberry Hollow.

Her eyes traveled down the text.

The deed referenced a large parcel of land that bordered the creek, stretching to the valley edge. The description was vague, old fashioned, filled with markers like "the leaning elm" and "the stone outcrop where the spring begins."

At the bottom, where signatures should have been, there was a space. A blank. The owner's name missing, as if someone had erased it decades ago.

Jenna leaned close. "What is that missing signature?"

Harriet shook her head. "No idea. But whoever removed it did not want anyone to know."

Mara looked again at the blank line.

"A deed with no owner," she whispered.

Ellie frowned. "That cannot be legal."

"Exactly," Harriet said. "If someone found this before Owen did... or if Owen found it and wanted to hide it, it would explain everything. It would explain the pressure. The fear. The secrecy."

Jenna tapped the edge of the paper.

"And the snowglobe," Jenna said. "Someone hid this clue inside the globe because they did not want Owen or anyone else to find it."

Mara stared at the paper, her pulse climbing.

"The miniature lantern," she murmured. "Iris always used lanterns in her globes to represent guidance. A path. A place to begin."

"That would make the rolled clue inside the snowglobe a starting point," Ellie said. "A hint. A message."

Mara nodded slowly, mind racing.

"It must have said something about the missing name," Mara whispered. "The paper Connor found. It must have referenced this deed. A clue to who the original owner was. Or who was meant to inherit it."

Harriet swallowed. "Owen wanted this land. All of it. The well. The creek. The abandoned parcel. He thought he could claim it for development if he could trace the deed history back far enough."

Jenna inhaled sharply. "So the missing signature ruins everything. Without that name, there is no legal transfer. No claim possible. Someone hid the clue to prevent him from taking control."

"And someone helped him search," Ellie said. "The gloved figure in your photos. The person near the side hallway."

Harriet closed her eyes.

"I think Owen was not working alone," Harriet whispered. "Someone was whispering in his ear. Someone who wanted the land just as much as he did... if not more."

Mara folded the deed carefully.

Her hands no longer shook.

She felt something steadier rising inside her. Something that had been buried under fear this whole time.

Resolve.

"I need to know what was written on the rolled paper inside the snowglobe," she said. "I need to understand what my aunt knew and why someone trusted her to hide it."

Ellie touched her arm. "Even if it leads to more danger?"

"It already has led to danger," Mara said. "It reached into my bakery. It reached into my life. It will not stop unless someone finds the truth."

Jenna nodded. "Then we do this together. We figure out why someone wanted this land so desperately they hid clues inside your work."

Harriet looked down at her gloves.

"I will go to Connor," Harriet said softly. "I will tell him everything. I should have done it sooner. I thought I was protecting the festival... but I was making things worse."

Mara shook her head. "You were trying to shield the town. That is not something to regret."

Harriet blinked rapidly, fighting tears.

"Iris would be proud of you," she said quietly. "You have her calm strength. I did not see it until now."

Those words struck something deep in Mara's chest.

For the first time since arriving in Frostberry Hollow, she let herself believe she belonged here. Not because of the bakery. Not because of her aunt. But because she was part of something bigger now, something important.

"We will find the missing name," Mara said. "We will find out why someone wanted to bury this deed. And we will find out who hid the clue in the snowglobe."

Harriet nodded.

"I will help in any way I can," she said.

The three women stood.

The library felt different now. Alive. A quiet guardian of the secrets they carried.

As they stepped outside again, the snowfall had eased. The air felt colder, but clearer. A path waited ahead, marked by clues and questions and shadows that Mara had no choice but to follow.

She walked between Ellie and Jenna, her breath rising in steady, determined clouds.

For the first time since Owen's collapse, Mara felt sure of one thing.

The snowglobe had not chosen her life at random.

Someone trusted Iris to hide the truth.

And now that truth had found its way to Mara.

She would uncover it.

All of it.

Piece by piece.

Starting with the missing name on the deed

and the lantern that had been taken from her snowglobe

to light the way forward.

* * *

The Frostberry Hollow Public Library sat tucked between the post office and the old historical museum, its stone steps brushed clean from the morning snowfall. Warm golden light glowed behind its tall windows, promising shelter from the cold. The familiar scent of cedar shelves and dusted books drifted into the entryway as Mara pushed open the heavy wooden door.

Ellie and Jenna walked quietly at her sides. All three moved with a shared tension, like musicians preparing to hold the same difficult note.

The library was mostly empty. A few college students huddled near the study tables, earbuds in and textbooks splayed out. An elderly man slept in a comfortable corner chair, a newspaper folded over his stomach. The librarian, Mrs.

Pineswell, looked up briefly and offered a gentle smile before returning to her cataloging.

Harriet Dove stood near the back wall, close to the section on local history. Her gloved hands clutched a manila envelope, and her coat was wrapped tightly around her, as if cold had seeped into her bones and refused to leave. When she saw Mara, relief flickered across her face, followed quickly by worry.

"Thank you for coming," Harriet whispered.

Mara gestured to the chairs near the corner reading nook. "We can talk over there."

They settled into the cluster of soft armchairs. The quiet hum of the library settled around them, making the moment feel strangely fragile.

Harriet exhaled shakily. "I do not know where to begin."

"Start with what you were going to tell me," Mara said gently.

Harriet looked down at the envelope in her lap.

"Owen gave me something last week," she said. "Something he wanted me to sign. Something that made no sense."

"What was it?" Ellie asked softly.

"A request," Harriet said. "A request to transfer partial oversight of a section of festival grounds to his company. He claimed it was for construction. Improvement. But I felt pressured. He wanted access to tunnels underneath the old pavilion, the part of the land the town has preserved since the mining era."

Mara froze.

"Tunnels," she whispered.

Ellie's eyes widened in recognition. "Connected to Tessa's land."

"And the old well," Jenna added quietly.

Harriet nodded. "I refused to sign. I told him he needed council approval. That made him furious. He said the town was full of people who had no vision."

Mara exchanged a glance with Jenna. "He said something similar to Tessa."

Harriet rubbed her forehead with trembling fingers.

"I thought it was bluster," Harriet said. "Owen always tried to get his way. But then two days ago I received a message from him asking for a private meeting after the brunch. He said the papers were urgent. Important. And that he had evidence he wanted to share with me."

Jenna leaned forward. "Evidence of what?"

Harriet hesitated.

"Evidence," she said slowly, "of land misallocation. Of missing deeds."

Silence swept over the group.

Mara felt her breath tighten. "Land deeds. Connor said the clue inside the snowglobe mentioned land."

Harriet's eyes widened. "Snowglobe?"

Mara nodded. "My snowglobe. The one from the auction. It was found in Owen's briefcase. Someone removed the lantern and hid a rolled paper inside."

Harriet's hand flew to her mouth.

"Oh my goodness," she whispered. "He was trying to show me something."

"Or someone did not want him to show you," Ellie said quietly.

Harriet lowered her hand and placed the manila envelope on the table.

"I could not bring myself to open this until now," she said. "But Owen dropped this envelope at the town office the day before the brunch. He said it contained council documents. He insisted I hold it until after the event."

"Do you think it is related?" Mara asked.

"I do not know," Harriet whispered. "But after hearing what you just told me, I cannot ignore it."

Her hands shook as she slid out a set of folded papers. She opened them slowly, smoothing them across her knees.

The document on top was an old map.

Frostberry Hollow. Dated over fifty years earlier.

Mara leaned closer. The map was covered in handwritten notes and inked borders, marking parcels of land with small numbers. Some sections were circled in red. Others were crossed out.

"That is the festival land," Jenna said, pointing to a central block. "And that is the pavilion. But look... the boundary lines are different."

Harriet nodded, her eyes tight. "They do not match current records."

Mara examined one of the red circled areas. "What is this section here?"

Ellie leaned closer. "That is behind Tessa's property."

"And this?" Jenna asked, pointing at a smaller block.

"That is Mark's building," Mara whispered.

Harriet lifted another page.

It was a deed transfer form. Unfinished. Never filed.

"Owen must have discovered these," Harriet said. "They indicate land parcels that were shifted years ago. Quietly. Without council approval. I had no idea. The records we have now reflect the changes, but this map shows what the land looked like before."

"And if land was moved or reassigned without oversight," Ellie said, "then someone benefited. A lot."

"Owen," Mara whispered. "Or someone he worked with. Or someone he was trying to expose."

Harriet looked at them with a haunted expression.

"This is not just political," Harriet said. "This is financial. This is legacy. Whoever was involved may have gained tens of thousands in property advantages."

Jenna tapped the map lightly. "And Owen hid the clue inside Mara's snowglobe. A place small, secret, and likely unnoticed."

Mara swallowed. "Why mine?"

Harriet's voice softened. "Your aunt, Iris, was trusted. People believed her snowglobes were safe spaces for memories. Maybe Owen thought the piece would not draw suspicion. Or maybe someone else used it without his knowledge."

Ellie gently reached across the table and squeezed Mara's hand.

"But the lantern inside," Ellie said. "Why remove it? And what did the paper say?"

"Owen never showed me," Harriet murmured. "But I think he expected to reveal everything after the brunch. Something big. Something he believed would change how the town sees their history."

Jenna broke the quiet.

"But someone stopped him."

The air tightened around them.

Harriet closed the folder slowly. "I should give this to Connor."

"Yes," Mara said. "But we also need to understand what we are looking at."

Harriet nodded. "Then we study it quickly. Before we turn it in."

They spread the papers across the table. The map, the misplaced deed, and several annotated notes that included numbers, initials, and dates.

Mara frowned at a marked section of the map.

"Look here," she said. "This ridge behind the old pavilion. The line cuts through the land in two different versions."

Ellie traced the border with her fingertip. "The boundary was expanded. Someone added land to one parcel that did not belong to it."

"And look at this," Jenna said, pointing at a handwritten note: "Fidelity discrepancy, 1972."

Harriet inhaled sharply. "That must be when the changes began."

Mara stared more closely.

Another inscription rested near the edge of the page.

It was tiny, almost faded.

But unmistakable.

"I know that handwriting," she whispered.

Ellie looked at her. "Whose is it?"

Mara felt her heart twist.

"My aunt's," she said softly. "Iris wrote this note."

The others fell still.

Harriet's eyes softened. "Oh, Mara."

Mara touched the faded words with gentle fingertips.

"She must have known something," Mara whispered. "She must have suspected what was happening. Maybe she made the snowglobe for someone connected to this. Or maybe she intended to hide something important."

Jenna shook her head slowly. "But she never told you."

"No," Mara murmured. "But she also never told me about the secret compartments in her early snowglobes. I only learned when I inherited her tools."

Harriet looked at the map again.

"This clue Owen carried," Harriet said softly, "it might be part of something Iris left behind."

Ellie nodded. "Something that was never meant to disappear."

Mara closed her eyes.

Her aunt's voice echoed faintly in memory, soft and warm, talking about town river paths and old stories. At the time Mara had thought nothing of it. Now those memories felt heavier, as if Iris had tried to speak through small moments she never fully explained.

"Iris must have tried to protect this town," Mara whispered. "And now someone is trying to protect their own secret. Or their family legacy."

"What do we do next?" Jenna asked.

Harriet gathered the papers.

"I will take these to Connor," Harriet said. "But you three must be careful. Whatever Owen discovered connects to people who have influence here. And at least one of them is desperate enough to break in and search your bakery."

Mara nodded. "I know."

Harriet stood, the folder held close to her chest again.

"I will call you after Connor sees the papers," Harriet said. "Until then, stay alert."

She left quietly, disappearing between the tall bookshelves.

Mara remained seated, staring at the spot where Harriet had stood.

Ellie touched her shoulder gently.

"We will get through this," Ellie said softly.

Jenna slid her chair closer. "We are in this with you. Start to finish."

Mara looked down at her hands, feeling a mixture of fear and determination swirling inside her chest like a winter storm.

"Whoever hid that clue inside my snowglobe," she said quietly, "wanted a secret about Frostberry Hollow to stay hidden."

Ellie nodded.

"And now we have to uncover it," Mara finished, her voice steadying.

Outside, snow drifted thickly past the windows, falling in steady waves across the quiet town. But inside Mara, something had changed. A new spark. A new resolve.

The snowglobe had returned.

The secret inside had surfaced.

And she was not going to stop until she understood every piece of it.

Chapter 12

Snow drifted across Frostberry Hollow in soft, powdery curtains as Mara and Ellie hurried toward the bakery's upper workroom. They had left Jenna at the counter to cover the late morning customers, though the bakery remained quiet enough that Jenna promised she would be fine for a while.

Mara climbed the stairs with the rolled paper in her hand, the same scrap Connor had shown her in the photograph. He had allowed her to look at it briefly under supervision, and what she remembered was enough to redraw the symbol by hand afterward. A crooked line. A half circle underneath. Three short vertical marks barely visible where age had rubbed the paper thin.

Once they reached the workroom, Mara closed the door behind them. The familiar scent of glue, varnish and wood polish wrapped around her like a memory of calmer days. Sunlight spilled through the frosted windowpane, casting pale rectangles across the tables scattered with snowglobe supplies.

Ellie pulled her coat off and paced the room, rubbing her arms.

"All right," Ellie said. "Let us see it again."

Mara laid the redraw on her worktable. Ellie leaned over, lowering her glasses to the tip of her nose as if the angle could reveal answers more clearly.

The symbol itself was tiny, about the size of a thumbnail, positioned on the lower corner of the reproduced clue. Mara had drawn it as precisely as she remembered. Every line. Every angle.

"Well," Ellie said, tapping a finger beside the mark, "this is not a common symbol. It does not look like a company logo. It does not resemble anything modern."

Mara nodded. "When I saw it at the sheriff's office, it felt older somehow. Like something from a different time."

"Older," Ellie repeated thoughtfully. "Perhaps too old for regular property paperwork."

Mara's pulse picked up. "You mean like... historic land deeds?"

Ellie did not smile, but her expression said the answer was yes.

"I think," Ellie said slowly, "that you have drawn an old miner's mark."

Mara straightened. "A miner's mark?"

"Yes," Ellie said. "Back when Frostberry Hollow was first founded, the area around the creek and the woods was scattered with mining claims. Workers marked the boundary of their staked claims with simple symbols. Many of them used whatever they could carve into stone or wood. Each miner had a unique mark."

Mara stared at the symbol again. The crooked line. The half circle. The three faint vertical strokes.

"So this could be a claim identifier," Mara said.

"More than could," Ellie said. "I have visited the town archives enough times to recognize a few of these symbols. This one belongs to a man named Elias Carrick. He staked one of the earliest claims outside Frostberry Creek Woods."

Mara felt a chill along her spine.

"Do you think the paper Connor found inside my snowglobe was referencing his claim?" she asked.

"Yes," Ellie said. "Or referencing someone else's attempt to claim what he left behind."

Mara pulled her chair closer to the worktable and sat slowly.

"What do we know about Elias Carrick?" she asked.

Ellie crossed her arms.

"I know his name shows up in several old record books," Ellie said. "He staked a mining plot in the late eighteen hundreds. Rumor says he found something unusual near Frostberry Creek before disappearing."

"Disappearing?" Mara repeated. "What sort of disappearance?"

"Well," Ellie said, "some stories say he left town. Others claim he vanished on his land. And a few say he recorded something in his journal that frightened him before he simply stopped showing up."

"Frightened him?" Mara whispered. "Why would a mining claim frighten someone?"

Ellie shrugged. "People were superstitious back then. But something must have happened. His claim changed hands twice after he disappeared, then vanished from most official records entirely. Only fragments remain."

"The symbol is one of those fragments," Mara said.

Ellie nodded.

Mara ran a fingertip lightly along her hand drawn reproduction, feeling the roughness of the pencil marks though she knew the original paper must have felt much older, almost brittle.

"Connor said the clue was tied to land deeds," Mara murmured. "He mentioned something missing from the historical files. Something no one has been able to trace."

"And now we know what it might be," Ellie said quietly.

Mara closed her eyes briefly.

"Elias Carrick's claim," she whispered.

Ellie inhaled slowly. "Yes. And that means Owen Barrow was either after something connected to that land... or trying to hide something about it."

Mara felt the weight of the statement settle deep in her chest.

"Owen pushed Tessa to sell her property," Mara said.

"Because of the well. Because of possible tunnels. What if those tunnels connect to the claim?"

Ellie sat down across from her. "It is a strong possibility."

"And Owen tried to evict Mark," Mara went on. "He wanted control over that entire strip of land near the creek. He even pressured Harriet about festival properties. Everything circles back to Frostberry Creek Woods."

Ellie nodded again, slowly.

"It does," she said. "The woods have been part of the town since the beginning. If the original claim lies somewhere in that area, it means controlling the surrounding land would give someone access to whatever Elias found."

Mara swallowed.

"We need to see the town's old records ourselves," she said. "If the symbol matches a mining claim, the archives might hold more."

"They might," Ellie agreed. "Or what is left of them might."

Mara stood, feeling a swell of nervous energy.

"I want to check the records today," she said. "Before someone else does."

Ellie rose as well.

"Then we go together," Ellie said firmly. "But you are taking gloves, a coat, and your sense of caution."

Mara gave a thin smile. "I can manage two out of the three."

Ellie fetched her own coat. "You will manage all three."

They made their way downstairs.

Jenna stood by the counter, typing on her laptop while keeping one eye on the door. At the sight of their serious faces, she closed the laptop immediately.

"Do we know something?" Jenna asked.

"Yes," Ellie said. "And we need to visit the archives."

Jenna grabbed her coat as well.

"Absolutely not without me," she said. "You two need someone who can charm a librarian or run a camera if things get interesting."

Mara blinked. "What sort of things do you expect?"

"With us?" Jenna said lightly. "Anything."

They stepped outside into the cold. Snow crunched beneath their boots as they walked toward the old brick building that housed the Frostberry Hollow municipal archives. It stood at the edge of the historic district, its stone foundation older than most of the town.

Inside, the air smelled faintly of aged paper and warm dust. Rows of shelves lined the space beneath dim lamps shaped like winter lanterns.

Mrs. Thompkins, the longtime archivist, looked up as they entered.

"Well," she said, "if it is not my favorite troublemakers."

"We are not troublemakers," Ellie insisted kindly. "We are concerned citizens with an interest in the past."

Mrs. Thompkins narrowed her eyes, though her smile betrayed her affection. "Concern often leads to curiosity, and curiosity leads to messes. What do you need this time?"

Mara stepped forward.

"Old mining claims," she said. "Specifically records tied to Elias Carrick."

Mrs. Thompkins froze.

Then she lifted one eyebrow.

"My, my," she said. "That name has not crossed my desk in years."

"Do you still have the records?" Mara asked.

Mrs. Thompkins sighed with theatrical weariness.

"Some," she said. "Not all. Several documents were lost in the fire of nineteen twenty. But a few pieces remain."

She led them to a long wooden table near the back and brought out a thin stack of weathered folders.

"Here you are," Mrs. Thompkins said. "Be gentle. These papers are older than half the buildings in this town."

Mara took the top folder carefully.

Inside were faded maps, hand sketched and crinkled with age. Claim charts. Boundary lines. Names scribbled across plots.

She scanned the pages until her breath caught.

"There," Mara whispered.

The symbol.

The crooked line. The half circle. The three faint vertical strokes.

Ellie and Jenna leaned in close.

"That is the same mark," Ellie said. "Elias Carrick."

Mara lifted the page closer to her face, her pulse quickening.

"And look," Jenna said softly. "The map shows the claim extending toward Frostberry Creek Woods."

"And the tunnels Tessa mentioned," Ellie added. "Probably part of the infrastructure the miners used."

Mara turned another page.

This one included a list of owners after Carrick. Two names had been crossed out. The third was incomplete, the name smudged beyond recognition.

The fourth line, written in cramped print, read:

Property transferred to F. B. Investments, 1964.

Mara frowned. "F. B. Investments?"

Ellie hissed sharply. "Frostberry Barrow Investments. Owen's family."

Jenna's eyes widened.

"Owen inherited the claim," Jenna whispered. "Or at least the rights to it."

Mrs. Thompkins leaned forward with interest.

New Year's Scone and the Missing Snowglobe (with recipes in the ...

"Ah yes," she said. "That name did show up from time to time. They managed several parcels near the creek."

Mara looked from the paper to Ellie and Jenna.

"Someone hid the clue inside my snowglobe," Mara said, voice trembling. "Someone wanted to expose the original claim. And Owen knew something was in the globe. That is why he took it."

Ellie squeezed Mara's hand.

"You are connecting the pieces," Ellie said. "It all points to one place."

Jenna inhaled.

"Frostberry Creek Woods," she said softly.

Mara looked at the map again, the old symbol pulsing in the dim light like a beacon.

The woods.

The claim.

The well on Tessa's property.

The tunnels beneath the land.

Owen pushing to buy neighboring properties.

The break in at the bakery.

Everything pointed to something hidden among the trees and the old earth, something someone wanted enough to steal her snowglobe and unearth a secret lost for generations.

Mara folded the map gently.

"We need to go to the woods," she whispered.

Ellie and Jenna exchanged looks.

"Not today," Ellie said. "Not without Connor knowing."

"Yes," Jenna added. "But soon. Very soon."

Mara held the folder close to her chest, feeling the weight of history in her arms.

Winter secrets lay buried beneath the snow.

And Frostberry Creek Woods waited.

Chapter 13

The next morning carried a low, heavy sky that promised more snow before dusk. Frostberry Hollow looked muted under the pale light, as if the town itself were holding its breath again. Mara walked toward the Old Mill Market with a growing mix of determination and dread, her boots crunching lightly along the icy path.

The wooden structure rose ahead, warm lights glowing behind fogged windows. Even from outside, the scents drifted into the street. Roasted nuts. Cloves. Winter citrus. It should have been comforting. Instead, it reminded her how many people here had secrets simmering right beneath the surface.

She pulled open the door.

The familiar bustle greeted her instantly. Vendors arranged displays. Customers wandered with steaming mugs. A child tugged on a parent's sleeve, pointing at the cookie stall. The hum of morning energy pulsed through the aisles.

And layered beneath it was the whispering.

Mara felt it the moment she stepped inside. Glances drifted her way. Conversations dipped. People knew something happened yesterday at the library. People always sensed when trouble sparked.

She steadied her breath and headed toward Mark Whitcomb's booth.

Mark was stacking candle jars, though his expression was distracted, as if his thoughts ran far ahead of his hands. When he looked up, surprise flickered across his face.

"Mara," he said. "Back again so soon."

"Yes," Mara replied gently. "I need to clarify something. It will not take long."

Mark set the jar down carefully.

"I figured you might come by," he said. "What do you need?"

She stepped close enough that their conversation remained private beneath the hum of the market.

"It is about the morning before the brunch," she said. "I need your memory exactly as it happened."

Mark's shoulders slumped a little. "I had a feeling this was coming."

"You said you saw Owen that morning," Mara reminded him. "At the market. You argued."

"Yes," Mark said quietly. "And I would take back that argument if I could."

She shook her head. "I am not here to judge. I need to know what he had with him. Anything unusual."

Mark hesitated, his gaze drifting to the stack of candle jars as if searching for courage.

"He was carrying something," Mark said finally. "An envelope."

Mara's breath caught.

"An envelope?" she repeated.

Mark nodded slowly.

"Thick," he said. "Like it held several folded pages. He kept it tucked inside his coat, but I saw him checking it when he thought I was not looking."

"Did he open it?" Mara asked.

"Not fully," Mark said. "But he glanced at the corner, like he was making sure it was still there."

Mara felt her pulse quicken. "Do you remember any markings on it?"

Mark frowned in concentration.

"Something on the front," he said. "I thought it was a smudge, but now that I think of it... it might have been a symbol. A shape. Not a word."

A shiver passed through her.

A symbol.

Like the marking on the rolled paper hidden inside her snowglobe.

Like the mining claim records she and Ellie had uncovered in the archives.

"Do you think anyone else saw him with it?" Mara asked.

Mark nodded.

"A few vendors noticed him pacing," he said. "He was not subtle. People pretended not to stare, but everyone felt on edge. Owen moved like he was expecting trouble."

"Was he alone the entire time?" Mara pressed.

"No," Mark whispered. "He talked to someone. Twice."

Mara leaned in. "Who?"

"I could not see the face," Mark said. "The person kept to the shadows near the pillar at the back. Dark coat. Dark scarf. Every time I looked, the person shifted away."

Mara felt her stomach tighten.

"Do you think it was the same person who met him at the brunch?" she asked softly.

Mark looked haunted. "I think it might be."

Mara pressed her hands together.

"Thank you," she said. "This helps more than you know."

Mark gave a sad half smile. "If I remember anything else, I will tell you. I promise."

Mara nodded and stepped back into the aisle.

As she moved deeper into the market, she felt eyes following her. She pretended not to notice, focusing on her next task: listening.

People talked in low voices as she passed. Half finished sentences. Nervous tones. Pieces of conversations thick with meaning.

At the fruit vendor's stand, two elderly women leaned close over bins of apples.

"I heard Owen came here looking for old maps," one whispered.

"No," the other replied. "He was asking about land boundaries. My cousin said so. Something about a forgotten claim."

Mara's chest tightened.

Maps.

Boundaries.

Claims.

Everywhere she turned, bits of conversation echoed things she and Ellie had found in the town archives.

She continued walking, weaving slowly through the stalls. The spice vendor spoke in a hushed tone to a man who looked like he had not slept well.

"He was here twice last week," the vendor murmured. "Wanted historical surveys. Who knows why."

A young woman at the craft counter whispered to her friend.

"My mom said he tried to buy a map of Frostberry Creek Woods from the historical board. Paid too much. She thought it was odd."

Frostberry Creek Woods.

Mara's breath hitched.

The same location marked on the old mining claim.

The same woods that bordered Tessa's land.

The same area where tunnels supposedly ran underground.

She continued walking, her senses sharpened.

At the jam stall, an older man adjusted jars with trembling fingers.

"I saw him near the back room," he said softly to his wife. "Talking to someone. He looked angry. And he kept patting his coat like he wanted to protect something inside."

"The envelope," Mara whispered to herself.

Every whisper, every murmur braided itself into the growing puzzle taking shape in her mind.

Owen had been desperate that morning.

Desperate... and afraid.

She turned the corner and nearly collided with Mrs. Kemple, who ran the dried herbs stall. The woman gasped, clutching her basket.

"Oh goodness, Mara. You startled me."

"Sorry," Mara said. "Are you all right?"

Mrs. Kemple gave a thin smile. "Just jumpy. Ever since the brunch... well, people feel unsettled. Strange things are happening."

Mara softened. "I know. I feel it too."

Mrs. Kemple lowered her voice.

"People say he met someone in the old supply corridor behind the market," she whispered. "Someone who asked him to bring that envelope."

Mara froze.

"Behind the market?" she whispered.

Mrs. Kemple nodded. "Yes. By the side door. The one no one uses unless they know the building well."

Mara's heart pounded.

A meeting.

A secret exchange.

Before the brunch.

Before the envelope changed hands again at the pavilion.

She thanked Mrs. Kemple, then stepped back, steadying her breath.

She had enough to bring Ellie and Jenna.

She left the market and hurried through the cold to the bakery. Snowflakes brushed her cheeks as she breathed in sharp, chilled air. The urgency pushed her forward until she reached the warm glow of the Cozy Nook Bakery.

Inside, Ellie and Jenna sat at the front table with steaming cocoa and a pile of papers between them.

They looked up as Mara entered.

"You look like you sprinted the whole way," Jenna said.

"I nearly did," Mara replied, brushing snow from her coat.

"Tell us everything," Ellie said. "Every detail."

Mara sat down, catching her breath. She looked at her friends, then started from the beginning.

"Mark saw Owen carry an envelope that morning," she said. "Thick. With a symbol on it."

Ellie's eyes sharpened. "The same symbol that matches the mining claim?"

"I think so," Mara said. "And Owen checked the envelope repeatedly, like he was afraid of losing it."

"And he spoke to someone," Jenna added, remembering the market rumors.

"Yes," Mara said. "And not just once. Mark said he saw Owen speak to someone near the back pillar. Other vendors overheard whispers about meetings in the supply corridor behind the market."

Ellie inhaled sharply.

"So he received something," Ellie said. "Then planned to deliver it, or hide it. Or both."

"And the snowglobe became part of the plan," Jenna added. "For hiding the clue."

Mara nodded, her thoughts racing.

"Owen was desperate," she said. "He was planning something. He knew the papers were valuable. And someone else wanted them badly enough to follow him."

Ellie leaned closer.

"Everything points to the land," Ellie whispered. "The old mining claim. The boundaries. Frostberry Creek Woods."

"And someone was willing to take any steps necessary to control it," Jenna said quietly. "Even if it meant taking something from your bakery. Or worse."

Mara stared at her hands.

The truth pressed closer now, its shape clearer than ever.

The snowglobe had not just been stolen.

It had been used.

Hidden.

Transported.

And hunted.

All because of the land.

And the land led straight toward Frostberry Creek Woods.

Mara lifted her gaze, feeling the weight of the realization settle in her chest.

"The answers are in those woods," she whispered. "That is where all the paths lead."

Ellie and Jenna exchanged a look.

Then Ellie reached across the table and clasped Mara's hand.

"Then that is where we go next," Ellie said softly.

The bakery felt very still.

Outside, the snow continued to fall.

Inside, the path forward became unmistakably clear.

Frostberry Creek Woods held the winter secrets they needed to uncover.

And Mara knew the next chapter of this mystery would take her into the heart of those shadows.

Chapter 14

The snow along Frostberry Hollow's eastern ridge fell thicker than usual that morning, drifting in soft swirls that brushed against rooftops and narrow fences. The air held a crisp sharpness, the sort that seemed to hush the entire town. Mara walked slowly along the path leading toward Tessa Barrow's house, her boots sinking slightly in the new powder. Her breath formed soft clouds that faded into the morning air.

The farther she walked, the more distant the bakery felt behind her. The town's bustle, the scent of cinnamon and coffee, the low murmur of customers' voices, all of it dissolved into quiet. Ahead of her lay Tessa's home, a small craftsman style cottage that sat half tucked beneath a grove of bare winter trees. Icicles hung from the porch roof, catching the light like slender glass ornaments.

Mara hesitated at the walkway.

She had spoken with Tessa many times, but this visit felt

different. Heavier. Something in Tessa's voice when she agreed to talk had sounded frayed, almost desperate.

Mara stepped forward and climbed the few porch steps. Before she could knock, the front door opened just enough for Tessa to peer out.

"You came," Tessa said quietly.

"I said I would," Mara replied.

Tessa stepped aside to let her in.

Inside, the house smelled faintly of eucalyptus and strong tea. The entryway opened into a modest living room filled with cozy mismatched furniture and several potted plants that should not have been thriving in winter, yet somehow were. Tessa's son, a lanky teenager with earphones slung around his neck, lingered by the hallway. He nodded once at Mara, polite but wary, then disappeared into his room without a word.

Tessa sighed.

"Sorry. He has been tense since the brunch."

Mara shook her head. "Please do not apologize. Everyone in town feels tense right now."

Tessa gestured toward the sofa.

"Sit," she said. "I made tea. It is calming. Or at least it claims to be calming. No guarantees."

Mara sat on the sofa while Tessa moved around the kitchen, returning moments later with two steaming mugs. She handed one to Mara, then sank into the armchair opposite her.

For a long moment they both sat quietly, the only sounds the ticking of a distant wall clock and the faint hum of the heater.

"You look tired," Tessa finally said.

"So do you," Mara replied softly.

Tessa gave a humorless smile. "I have barely slept. Too many thoughts. Too many possibilities. And I am afraid of choosing the wrong one."

Mara wrapped her hands around the warm mug.

"You asked me to come," she said gently. "You said there was more I needed to know."

Tessa stared into her tea as if searching for courage.

"Yes," she said. "But I need to start at the beginning. No shortcuts."

Mara nodded, patient.

Tessa took a breath.

"When you asked about Owen's plans for my land," she began, "I told you only a fraction of what happened. Not because I wanted to hide it, but because I did not know how much of it mattered. Now I think all of it matters."

"What changed your mind?" Mara asked.

"The snowglobe," Tessa said. "And what was inside it. And the fact that the clue mentioned land."

Mara felt a chill crawl along her arms.

Tessa leaned forward.

"The well on my property," she continued. "It is not just an old well. It was used during the mining days. Most people forgot it existed, but Owen did not. He asked about it, insisted that I allow him access, told me it was unsafe and needed to be filled. Then he changed his story and claimed it could be made useful."

"Useful how?" Mara asked.

Tessa shook her head.

"He never said exactly. But he offered more money than the land was worth. A ridiculous amount. Enough to make anyone suspicious."

"Why did you refuse?" Mara asked softly.

"Because his interest was not normal," Tessa said. "Because his smile never reached his eyes. Because he talked like everything in this town already belonged to him. And because..." She hesitated. "Because the land has been in my family for generations. My grandparents used to talk about it as if it were more than soil."

Mara leaned in. "More than soil?"

Tessa looked down at her hands.

"My grandmother said there was a time when owning certain land in Frostberry Hollow meant owning the stories beneath it," she said. "I never knew what that meant. I thought it was old family superstition. But now..."

"You think Owen wanted what was beneath your land," Mara whispered.

"I know he did," Tessa said. "And he tried everything to get it."

Tessa's voice shook slightly. Mara waited, giving her space.

"Two weeks ago," Tessa continued, "he came to the house with a file folder. He said it contained records about land transfers from the early days of the town. Mining rights, water rights, old ownership claims. He said my land was part of something larger, and that he was the rightful successor to that claim."

Mara frowned. "Did you look inside the folder?"

"No," Tessa admitted. "I was too angry. Too overwhelmed. I told him to take the folder and leave. But he refused. Said he would give me proof in time."

"And did he?" Mara asked.

Tessa shook her head. "No. Instead, he sent someone else."

Mara blinked. "Who?"

"A woman," Tessa said. "She came by three days before the brunch. She was polite. Controlled. She said she represented Owen's development interests and needed to verify the boundaries of my land."

"Do you know her name?" Mara asked.

"No," Tessa said. "She did not give it."

Mara exhaled slowly. More layers. More shadows.

"Why are you telling me this now?" Mara asked gently.

Tessa set her mug down, her expression tightening with an emotion Mara could not name.

"Because I think Harriet might be involved," Tessa said. "And I think you are one of the only people who can connect the pieces."

Mara froze.

"Harriet?" she repeated. "You think Harriet had something to do with Owen's pressure tactics? Or with his death?"

Tessa's jaw clenched.

"She knew about his land claims," Tessa said. "She knew he wanted to buy property and reorganize festival grounds. She was at the center of every town decision he tried to influence. And she was angry. Very angry."

"But that does not mean she did anything wrong," Mara said carefully.

Tessa looked away.

"You do not understand," she said. "Harriet is careful. She smiles at everyone. But she carries grudges like stones in her pockets. I have known her since childhood. She never forgets when someone stands in her way."

Mara felt her pulse quicken.

"But what proof do you have?" she asked.

Tessa hesitated.

"I do not have proof," Tessa admitted. "Just a feeling. A memory. And what she said to me last week. Something that sounded innocent then, but now feels important."

"What did she say?" Mara asked quietly.

Tessa met her eyes.

"She said Owen was playing with fire," Tessa whispered. "And she hoped he remembered that land can burn."

Mara's breath caught.

"And then she said," Tessa continued, "that some things buried should stay buried."

Silence hung heavy between them.

Mara sipped her tea, needing the warmth to steady herself.

"Tessa," she said softly, "you are hurting. You are frightened. And I understand why. But right now, we cannot accuse Harriet without something solid. Not when the town is already tangled in panic."

Tessa pressed her palms together.

"I know," she said quietly. "But I needed to tell someone. You deserve to know how deep this goes."

Mara nodded slowly.

"I believe you," she said. "I believe everything you told me. But we must be careful."

Tessa looked down, relieved but tense.

"I do not want to blame the wrong person," Tessa whispered. "But I cannot shake the feeling that Harriet knows something. Something she has not told the sheriff."

Mara reached across the space between them and rested a hand on Tessa's.

"We will find the truth," she said. "Piece by piece. Even if it is buried under snow and stories."

Tessa nodded once, a tear slipping down her cheek before she swiped it away.

In that moment, Mara saw something she had missed before.

This was not just about land.

Not just about ownership.

It was about people whose lives had been pushed, pressured, and pulled apart by Owen Barrow's ambition.

And someone in town had decided enough was enough.

Mara felt the weight of the realization settle in her chest.

This was not just a mystery.

This was a conflict simmering beneath Frostberry Hollow for years.

And the truth, whatever it was, would not be gentle.

Tessa led Mara through the narrow hallway to a small sitting room filled with old framed photographs and shelves lined with mismatched books. The wood stove in the corner crackled softly, filling the room with a gentle heat that contrasted with the heaviness of the conversation.

A crocheted blanket lay folded across the back of the couch, and a stack of children's artwork sat on the low coffee table.

Tessa hesitated before moving a drawing aside, as if it mattered more to her than she wanted to admit.

Mara sat carefully on the edge of the couch, her palms flat against her knees.

"Tessa," she said quietly. "I want to understand. You said Owen tried to buy your land. I know that much. But now I need to know why this was so personal for you."

Tessa lowered herself into a chair across from her. She twisted her hands together for a long moment before she spoke.

"In this town," Tessa said, "people think they know your life just because they know your name. But that is not true. Most of what matters in a person's story is buried under everything they hide."

Mara nodded slowly. "I believe that."

Tessa looked toward the window, her gaze distant.

"My parents lived on that land," she said. "My grandparents too. They kept the old well sealed because they did not trust what might be beneath it. They said certain tunnels were better forgotten. They said the land was safe as long as it stayed in the family."

Mara felt a shiver crawl up her spine.

"And then," Tessa continued, "when my parents passed, everything fell to me. The house. The land. The debt. And Owen showed up three months later with offers that sounded like threats covered in sugar. He said he could help me. He said I was drowning and he had the only rope."

"He really believed he could take anything he wanted," Mara said softly.

Tessa let out a bitter laugh. "He did not just believe it. He depended on it. He had me cornered. He told me if I did not sell, he would find a way to make the town zoning board reconsider my rights to the property. He said he could claim parts of it for future development. He hinted at old documents that might prove the land belonged to someone else decades ago."

Mara blinked. "Old documents. Like land deeds."

Tessa nodded sharply. "Yes. Old maps. Old transfers. He talked about them as if he already had them, or knew where they were hidden. It made me wonder if he had found something I did not know existed."

Mara leaned forward. "And this is what he was doing before the brunch? Pressuring you again?"

Tessa nodded. "He came to the market yesterday morning and told me I should consider a different path. That if I did not choose to sell peacefully, other people might get involved."

Mara felt a chill. "Other people like who?"

Tessa shrugged with frustration. "He never said. Just implied. Owen liked to let his threats hang like icicles over your head."

"Did he say anything that connected to Harriet?" Mara asked carefully.

Tessa's jaw tightened.

"I think he did," she said. "But not directly. Harriet has been arguing with him for years over festival planning, over town projects, over funding. She always said she wanted the community protected from developers like him."

"That is not the same as being involved," Mara said gently.

Tessa looked away. "Maybe not. But she met with him a few times last month. Privately. I saw them at the café together. Twice."

Mara frowned. "That does not mean she was helping him."

"No," Tessa said quietly. "But she cared about the future of the town. And she needed money. Owen had money. Sometimes that combination ruins people."

Mara studied Tessa closely. "Are you trying to say Harriet might have helped him? Or wanted something from him?"

Tessa sighed, shoulders sagging.

"I do not know," she admitted. "I keep trying to understand all the pieces. And I keep finding reasons to doubt everyone."

Mara felt an ache bloom behind her ribs.

"Are you sure this is not about something else?" Mara asked gently. "Something more personal than land or money?"

Tessa's eyes glistened in the light of the wood stove.

"I have spent years trying to protect what is mine," she whispered. "I raised two children alone. I worked double shifts every week. I barely slept. My land was the one thing I had left that belonged to my family. And Owen tried to rip it out from under me like it was nothing."

Silence settled between them.

Slow. Heavy.

Tessa wiped at her eyes quickly, as if refusing to let tears fall.

"I hated him for that," she admitted. "I hated what he represented. The way he smiled while hurting people. The way he made me feel small."

Mara inhaled softly. "Anger is not the same as guilt."

"I know," Tessa said. "But I was desperate. And desperate people do stupid things."

Mara felt the room tilt with tension.

"What stupid things?" she asked quietly.

Tessa shook her head. "Not violence. Never that. But I might have said things. Harsh things. I told him he would regret pushing me. I told him secrets never stayed buried, not even under snow."

Mara's breath caught.

"That sounds like something Owen would not ignore."

"No," Tessa said softly. "He did not ignore it."

Mara waited.

"He came to my house," Tessa continued. "The day before the brunch. Holding that same black envelope I saw in Jenna's photo. He said he had changed his mind. He said he wanted to offer me a temporary deal. Something to tide me over until he could make a better long term proposal."

Mara blinked. "A temporary deal? Regarding what?"

"My land," Tessa whispered. "Or part of it."

"Did you accept?"

"No," Tessa said quickly. "I slammed the door in his face."

Mara pressed a hand to her heart.

"Tessa," she said softly, "you were right to protect yourself."

Tessa shook her head, her expression conflicted.

"I do not know what is right anymore," she said. "I keep wondering if I should have listened to him. If the old well really did matter. If he found something that could change the entire ownership of this valley."

Mara swallowed.

"And Harriet?" she asked gently.

Tessa looked away. "Harriet might know more than she wants to admit. She always had paperwork. She always had access to archived deeds. I just cannot prove anything. But if someone was hiding documents inside your snowglobe, someone else was trying to find them."

Mara closed her eyes for a moment, overwhelmed by the sheer tangle of motives.

When she opened them again, Tessa was looking at her with a mix of fear and hope.

"I did not hurt him," Tessa said quietly. "I swear to you, Mara. But something is happening beneath this town, and it is not just about Owen Barrow. It is about history. Ownership. Secrets people wanted forgotten."

Mara nodded slowly.

"And now," Tessa said, voice trembling, "those secrets are trying to claw their way back to the surface."

The room grew very still.

Outside, the wind pressed softly against the windows, as if listening.

Inside, Mara realized that the conflict was not just business competition.

It was personal. Deeply personal.

And someone in Frostberry Hollow had been willing to risk everything to keep the past hidden.

* * *

Mara sat quietly in Tessa's living room as the weight of the last confession settled into the quiet. A log cracked softly in the fireplace, sending a small cascade of sparks upward. Outside, Frostberry Hollow lay under a deepening curtain of snowfall, the windows blurring as winter pressed against the glass.

Tessa had begun pacing again, rubbing her palms against her sleeves as if trying to scrape away memories that clung too tightly.

"I know what it sounds like," Tessa said. "I know I look like someone trying to blame Harriet just to save myself. But you have to understand something, Mara. Owen did not just want my land. He wanted control. And Harriet knew about several of those attempts. She was not innocent."

Mara breathed in slowly, trying to ground herself in the warmth of the room. "Not innocent does not mean responsible," she said softly.

Tessa turned sharply. "You did not hear them arguing two weeks ago."

"Arguing about what?"

"The festival land," Tessa said. "Owen threatened to pull his funding if Harriet did not support one of his development plans. She refused. She told him the town did not belong to him. He said something like, money always wins eventually. It was ugly. I heard every word."

Mara pressed her hands together. She could imagine Harriet trying to keep a polite face while Owen jabbed at her pride. She could also imagine Harriet refusing to bend. But imagining was not the same as knowing. And knowing was the fragile thread Mara needed.

"Do you think Harriet would have harmed him?" Mara asked carefully.

Silence thickened between them.

Tessa sat down slowly, as if her legs could no longer keep her upright.

"I do not know," she said. "That is the truth. I do not know. But I do know she is capable of pushing back harder than people think. She pressures people quietly. She corners them with rules and favors. She knows the shape of every secret in this town."

"That does not make her a killer," Mara said gently.

Tessa covered her face with both hands. "I know. I know that. But Owen was ruining everything for so many people. And someone snapped."

Mara breathed out, long and slow.

"And the snowglobe?" Mara asked. "Where does Harriet fit into that?"

Tessa hesitated.

"I cannot prove this," she said, "but Harriet was the last one I saw adjusting the auction table before people arrived. She moved things. She touched the snowglobe. She said she wanted the display to look balanced."

"That is not unusual for Harriet," Mara said. "She is a perfectionist."

"She had the gloves," Tessa murmured. "The ones Daniel mentioned. The ones in Jenna's photo. She was near Owen before the brunch. She was near the hallway. She had motive. She had opportunity. And she definitely had something to gain if he fell out of the picture."

Mara felt the familiar pressure of too many puzzle pieces gathering at once. Some fit. Some did not. Some felt like they belonged to an entirely different puzzle altogether.

"Tessa," Mara said quietly, "you are grieving and angry and scared. Everyone is. But pointing to Harriet without solid proof only creates new damage."

Tessa nodded weakly. "That is why I have not gone to Connor. I do not trust my judgment right now."

Mara's heart softened. She moved to sit beside Tessa on the couch.

"You are not wrong for noticing things," Mara said. "And you are not wrong for wanting justice. But anger is not enough to solve this. We need clarity."

The wind shifted outside, rattling a loose shutter somewhere along the side of the house. The sound felt eerie in the otherwise intimate quiet.

Tessa took a shaky breath. "There is something else."

Mara turned to her. "What is it?"

Tessa rose again, walked to a small desk near the window, and pulled open a drawer. From inside she took a thin folder tied with a frayed piece of twine.

"I found this in my mailbox last night," Tessa said. "No return name. No explanation. Just this."

Mara felt her pulse jump.

"What is inside?" she asked.

Tessa loosened the twine and opened the folder. Several photocopied pages lay inside. Handwritten notes in the margins. Old survey maps. And a highlighted line that made Mara's breath catch.

"Property transfers near Frostberry Creek Woods," Tessa said. "Do you see what it says?"

Mara took the top page, scanning the text.

Her voice came out faint.

"These deeds have never been legally filed…"

"Yes," Tessa said. "And the signatures listed are fake. Someone tried to claim areas near the creek without proper approval."

Mara turned to the next page. More highlighted sections. More irregularities. More evidence of attempts to obtain land through back channels.

"Owen was involved," Tessa whispered. "His name is on several drafts. He wanted control of the creek access. He believed something was buried there. Something connected to the old mining claim. Something valuable."

Mara stared at the papers.

"Where did these come from?" she asked softly.

Tessa shook her head. "I do not know. They were left for me. Maybe someone thought Owen threatened me enough that I should have them. Maybe someone wanted to lead me toward Harriet. Or away from someone else."

Mara set the papers down, her thoughts tumbling like snow tumbling off a roof.

"The clue inside the snowglobe mentioned land deeds," Mara said. "These documents show irregularities with land deeds. Someone hid these to protect themselves. Or to expose someone else."

Tessa lowered her head. "I did not know how deep he was involved. I thought he was just greedy. But this… this is bigger."

Mara felt a chill slip through her.

"It ties back to something old," she whispered. "The mining claim. The well. The creek access. Trails that have been there longer than any of us."

Tessa shivered. "I hate that he dragged the whole town into this."

Mara touched her hand gently. "You did not cause this. You only lived too close to the danger."

Tessa nodded slowly, tears beginning to gather in her eyes.

Mara looked toward the window. The falling snow blurred the trees, their branches swaying like muted shadows.

"This is no longer just about Owen," Mara whispered. "Someone else set these wheels in motion. Someone still moving behind the scenes."

Tessa breathed out softly, wiping her cheeks.

"What will you do now?" she asked.

Mara felt something settle inside her. Not calm exactly. Not confidence. But clarity. A small flicker of understanding.

"I will talk to Connor," Mara said. "I need to show him these papers. And I need to tell him what you witnessed. But I will not accuse Harriet. Not yet."

Tessa nodded. "Thank you for that."

Mara gathered the folder gently.

"And Tessa," she added softly, "someone left these documents for a reason. Be careful. Someone may want you to look one way so you do not look another."

Tessa closed her eyes. "I know."

Mara rose, pulling her coat around her like a shield.

As she stepped toward the door, she glanced back. Tessa stood in the center of her living room, small against the wide window, framed by snow falling behind her.

The emotional toll was written plainly in her shoulders. Whatever Owen had been doing, the damage had reached far beyond him, settling into places where it did not belong.

Mara stepped outside. The cold nipped at her cheeks. The pathway was already covered again with fresh snow. For a moment she lingered, looking back at Tessa's house, at the tired glow in the windows.

Then she walked down the path, the folder held against her chest, the weight of it heavy with secrets.

Winter pressed against Frostberry Hollow, carrying more stories than anyone had realized.

Mara knew now that she was walking through the center of something old, tangled, and dangerous.

And she had no choice but to keep going.

* * *

Snow began falling again as Mara left Tessa's living room, soft flakes drifting past the wide front windows. The storm had begun almost imperceptibly, as if the sky had needed time to collect everything unsaid in the room and cloak it in white.

Tessa stood by the fireplace, arms crossed tightly, watching Mara as if afraid she might break apart on the walk home. Her earlier fierceness had dimmed, softened into something brittle.

"I did not mean to lash out," Tessa said quietly. "I know Harriet might not be involved. I am just tired. Tired of his pressure. Tired of being pushed and ignored and spoken over."

Mara slipped into her coat slowly. "You are allowed to feel tired. None of this has been simple."

Tessa let out a shaky breath. "I do not want to be the villain. I do not want my name whispered in town as someone who hated him. But I did hate him sometimes. I hated the way he made me feel small on my own land."

Mara stepped closer, resting a gentle hand on Tessa's arm.

"Hating someone difficult does not make you guilty of anything," Mara said softly. "It makes you human."

Tessa blinked hard, tears forming but refusing to fall. She looked away, jaw tightening, the fight returning to her shoulders even as the vulnerability clung there too.

"I want this to end," she said. "I want his shadow gone from my life. I want the well on my land to stay a harmless story, not a target. I want people to stop asking what I knew."

"They ask because they are scared," Mara said. "But fear clouds judgment. It does not define truth."

For a long moment they stood in the soft glow of the fire,

neither speaking, both listening to the wind nudge at the windows.

At last Tessa nodded, swallowing hard. "If you find out anything that clears this fog, please tell me. Even if it is something I do not want to hear."

"I will," Mara promised.

She reached for the door, hesitated, and looked back.

"Tessa," she said, "there is something I need to ask you. When Owen talked about your property, did he ever mention the woods along Frostberry Creek?"

Tessa's brows lifted. "Frostberry Creek Woods? Only that the land near the water has older survey lines than most people realize. He said the records were messy. Why?"

Mara's pulse gave a faint skip. She tried to hide the uneasy spark that lit inside her.

"I have seen something connecting him to those woods," she said. "Old claims, old deeds, strange markings."

Tessa absorbed this with a slow, thoughtful frown.

"If Owen was chasing something in those woods," she murmured, "it must have been old. Something he thought was worth a fight."

"Or worth hiding," Mara said.

Tessa sighed. "Be careful. Secrets buried in this town tend to belong to people who do not like losing them."

"I know," Mara said. "But I cannot ignore what is unfolding."

She stepped out into the cold, the door closing with a soft click behind her. The snow kissed her cheeks as she walked, gentle at first, then thicker as the wind began to swirl it around her coat.

Mara tightened her scarf and moved down Tessa's front path, feeling the weight of everything she had learned settle heavier than the snow itself.

Owen's secret sales.

The unexplained bids for land.

The pressure on Mark.

The obsession with Tessa's property.

The missing snowglobe.

The symbol on the hidden paper pointing to old claims by Frostberry Creek.

It was no longer a collection of scattered clues. They were threads woven through the town, tied to places people walked past every day, unaware of the history simmering beneath the surface.

She paused at the end of the driveway, staring toward the woods visible beyond the distant rooftops. Their dark silhouette rose against the white horizon like a quiet sentinel.

People in Frostberry Hollow spoke often of winter magic. Of the safety of small towns. Of the peace tucked into snow covered evenings.

But now, Mara could only think of secrets hidden beneath roots and frost.

Secrets someone had killed to protect.

Secrets someone might kill again to keep hidden.

Her breath fogged the air as a realization, slow and steady, sank deep into her bones.

This was no longer just about proving her innocence or saving her bakery.

She had stepped into a legacy of concealed histories that began long before Owen Barrow. A conflict tied to the land itself. The town's past. Its foundations. Its quiet corners.

And Frostberry Creek Woods waited at the center of it, silent and watchful.

Mara drew her coat tighter around her and began the walk back into town. The snowfall thickened behind her, erasing her footprints almost as quickly as she made them.

The conflict was not just political. Not just financial.

It was personal.

For Tessa.

For Mark.

For Harriet.

And now, deeply and undeniably, for her.

Chapter 15

The evening snowfall had thickened into a slow, steady white curtain by the time Mara locked the bakery doors. The streetlamps outside cast soft halos through the drifting flakes, turning the world into a quiet winter lantern. The town looked hushed and contemplative, as if Frostberry Hollow itself were listening closely to secrets whispered across its snowy rooftops.

Inside the bakery, the warm lights glowed against the windows, and the air carried the faint scent of cooling vanilla and cinnamon. Mara moved slowly, her muscles weighed down by the day's discoveries. She cleaned the counter without really seeing it, her mind replaying everything that had happened.

The symbol on the clue.

The mining claim.

Owen's involvement.

Harriet's early presence at the pavilion.

And now... unanswered questions, growing heavier by the hour.

The bell on the door jangled suddenly.

Mara startled, heart jumping into her throat.

Jenna rushed inside, bundled in her thick green coat, curls dusted with snow, cheeks flushed with urgency.

"I came straight over," Jenna said, breath puffing in small clouds. "You have to see these."

Mara blinked. "Photos?"

"Yes," Jenna said, already digging into her bag. "I was sorting through the remaining brunch images, the ones I took before everything happened. I missed these earlier because they were in my backup card."

Jenna pulled out her camera, set it on the table, and connected it to her laptop. Her fingers trembled slightly as she clicked through the files.

"Sit," Jenna urged.

Mara sat slowly, her pulse quickening.

Jenna brought up the first photo.

It showed the Ice Pavilion, but the lights were dimmer. Decorations half set up. Chairs not yet arranged. Tables not completely prepared.

This was before the event even opened.

And there in the foreground, standing near the auction table, was Harriet Dove.

Mara leaned closer.

"Look at the time stamp," Jenna whispered.

Mara read it.

"That is nearly an hour before volunteers were scheduled to arrive."

"Yes," Jenna said. "And she looks like she is checking something. Look at her hands."

Harriet was turned partly away from the camera, but her posture revealed focused concentration. One hand seemed to be adjusting something on the auction table, while the other hovered near the spot where the snowglobe had eventually been placed.

"There is no snowglobe yet," Mara whispered.

"Exactly," Jenna said. "But she is paying attention to that exact part of the table. Before anything was there. Before anyone else got there."

A prickling feeling crawled up Mara's spine.

"Harriet said she arrived on time," Mara murmured. "She did not say she was there early. And she did not mention checking that area."

"Mara," Jenna said softly. "I do not want to accuse her of anything. But there is something strange about this."

Mara nodded slowly.

"Show me the other photo," she said.

Jenna hesitated. "This one is harder."

She clicked forward.

Mara's breath caught at once.

The second image was grainy, slightly blurred, taken from a distance. But the scene was unmistakable.

It was the shadowed hallway corner from the brunch. The one where Mara had seen Owen speaking to someone. The one where the envelope exchange had taken place.

And in this photo, the angles captured the moment differently.

Not clearer. But more revealing.

The gloved hand was still partly hidden. The dark wool sleeve still visible. But this time the figure leaned just slightly out of the shadows.

Enough to show the faint outline of a shoulder. The curve of a coat collar. The shape of the stance.

It was not proof. Not a face. Not an identity.

But it was far closer than the earlier images.

Mara's hand tightened around the table edge.

"This is the moment from chapter seven," Mara whispered. "The envelope exchange."

"Yes," Jenna said. "I did not even know I captured it twice. I must have taken a burst and accidentally deleted half of them from my main card. This one survived on the backup."

Mara stared at the figure. The posture. The height. The way their weight leaned slightly to the right.

A cold realization pressed at her throat.

"It looks familiar," she whispered. "Not clear. But familiar."

"Same coat?" Jenna asked.

"Possibly," Mara said. "But the light is too dim. I cannot be certain."

Jenna studied Mara carefully.

"What do you make of it?"

"I do not know," Mara said quietly. "But if Harriet was there early, and she had the right gloves, and she knew about the land issues, then…"

She did not finish the thought.

She did not have to.

The bakery felt colder suddenly, despite the warm lights.

A soft knock at the door made both women jump.

Mara stood slowly and peered through the window.

Sheriff Connor Hale stood outside, snow settling on his shoulders. He looked tired, the kind of tired that came from too many unanswered questions.

Mara unlocked the door and let him inside.

Connor brushed snow from his jacket and looked between the two women.

"I saw the lights," he said. "I figured you might still be here."

"You have news?" Mara asked.

Connor nodded once, the motion slow and deliberate.

"I came to warn you," he said. "Not to question you."

Mara's pulse skipped.

"What does that mean?" she asked, sitting again.

Connor looked at Jenna, then at Mara.

"The situation with the snowglobe is escalating," he said. "The clue inside it appears to relate to several properties Owen planned to acquire. Some of those transactions look suspicious. Possibly illegal. Possibly forged."

Mara felt the blood drain from her face.

"And because the clue was hidden in something you made," Connor continued, "people may start drawing conclusions. Wrong conclusions."

Jenna bristled. "That is not fair."

"I know," Connor said. "But fear rarely listens to fairness. Rumors already began spreading at the town hall meeting tonight."

Mara held her breath. "About me?"

"About you, and about who Owen trusted," Connor said gently. "And about who may have been involved in hiding or stealing documents connected to his land dealings."

Jenna's eyes widened. "Harriet."

Connor frowned slightly. "I cannot speak to that yet. What I can tell you is this. If you continue digging into this on your own, you may interfere with the investigation. Or put yourself in danger."

"I am already in danger," Mara whispered.

Connor paused.

"You are not wrong," he said quietly. "Someone broke into your bakery. Someone searched your tools. Someone stole the snowglobe. Someone hid evidence inside it. Whoever that person is, they have already crossed too many lines."

Mara's heartbeat thudded in her ears.

"So what are you saying?" she asked.

Connor set his hands on the table, leaning forward slightly.

"I am saying step back," he said. "Leave this to me now. Let the investigation run its course. I know you want answers, but I cannot protect you if you keep walking right into the middle of this."

Mara met his eyes.

For a moment, neither spoke.

The snowfall outside pressed a soft hush against the windows, deepening the stillness between them.

"I cannot step back," Mara said softly.

Connor closed his eyes briefly.

"Mara…"

"I have to keep going," she said. "The snowglobe belonged to me. My aunt taught me this craft. Whoever hid that clue chose her work. My bakery was searched. My tools touched.

Someone thinks I am part of this, or that I know something. I cannot live with this hanging over my life and do nothing."

Jenna nodded fiercely beside her. "We are in this now. Whether we wanted to be or not."

Connor straightened slowly.

"I was afraid you would say that," he murmured.

Mara crossed her hands tightly.

"But I will be careful," she said. "I promise. I will not confront anyone alone. I will call you if something happens. But I need to understand this. I need to know why my snowglobe was chosen. And what the clue really means."

Connor looked torn, frustration woven through concern.

Finally, he nodded once.

"Then be smart," he said. "Be cautious. And do not trust anyone too quickly."

His gaze lingered on her, carrying a weight she felt deep in her chest.

Then he pulled his coat closed and stepped toward the door.

"Good night, Mara," he said quietly. "Call me if anything changes."

She watched him walk away, his figure vanishing into the snowfall.

Jenna exhaled shakily.

"He is right," she whispered. "You should step back."

"Yes," Mara said, her voice barely above a whisper.

But she did not mean it.

Her hands tightened into fists.

"The truth is close," she said. "I can feel it. And someone out there knows it too."

Jenna nodded slowly. "And that someone is getting nervous."

Mara looked toward the snowy street outside. A single streetlamp flickered in the gentle wind, casting a trembling golden glow across the quiet walkway.

"Nervous people make mistakes," Mara whispered. "And whoever touched my snowglobe... they have made one already."

The winter night pressed in around the bakery, soft but unyielding. Outside, the town slept under a blanket of white.

Inside, Mara felt a calm resolve settle through her.

She would not be intimidated.

She would not step back.

And she would not let her aunt's craft be used for secrets without revealing why.

The mystery was winding tighter.

But Mara Linden was no longer afraid of the dark corners of Frostberry Hollow.

She was ready to walk straight into them.

Chapter 16

Morning crept into Frostberry Hollow with a quiet softness that did little to calm Mara's nerves. Pale sunlight filtered through thin clouds, spreading a faint glow across the snow piled outside the bakery windows. The world looked peaceful from the outside, but Mara felt a persistent pull of tension along her spine, a whispering reminder that things were unraveling beneath the surface.

She stepped into the bakery early, before Ellie or Jenna arrived, before the ovens warmed the shop. Everything felt colder at this hour, the quiet carrying an uneasy echo. She set her bag on the counter and went straight to the storage room where she had kept the evidence Connor returned to her earlier, the one piece of the snowglobe the sheriff permitted her to keep for examination.

The swapped miniature lantern.

It sat in a small padded box on her worktable, looking deceptively ordinary. The lantern was only an inch tall, the tiny painted surface smooth under her fingertips. It was heavier than normal for its size, weighted at the bottom like someone had modified it intentionally. Mara lifted it carefully, her breath catching as light glinted off the delicate curve of the tiny metal frame.

She turned it over in her hand.

The base had faint lines where someone had pried it open or reattached it. Not marks made by her. Not marks belonging to her aunt either. These marks were purposeful, but unskilled. Someone who knew just enough to attempt something complicated, but not enough to hide the evidence perfectly.

Mara frowned at the glue residue near the base. It was slightly amber toned, thicker than typical craft glue.

"I know this," she whispered.

Her aunt Iris had been a master of miniature adhesives. Some glues were too thick, some too runny, some yellowed with age or were too brittle in winter temperatures. But Iris had developed a preference for a rare specialty glue sold only in a handful of artisan shops. It was expensive. It had a distinctive scent. And it dried amber.

Mara leaned closer, inhaling slowly.

Yes.

This glue was one she had smelled hundreds of times growing up. It was the one Iris used for delicate repairs and hidden compartments, the glue she reserved for pieces that required precision and strength.

A chill spread down Mara's arms.

She pulled one of Iris's old instruction notebooks from a shelf, flipping through sketches and notes until she found a familiar scribble.

Miniature repairs. Secret hinge sealing. Do not use common craft glue. Use amber binding instead.

Mara set the notebook down.

Someone had used her aunt's preferred glue to alter the lantern. Someone who knew about snowglobe construction. Someone who cared about hidden compartments. Someone who had learned from Iris or watched her work long enough to understand the materials.

Her breath trembled.

"Who knew her techniques?" Mara whispered.

The list was smaller than it should have been.

Iris had been private about her craft. Most townspeople admired her work but did not understand how it was made. Only a handful of people had spent time with Iris in her workspace. Mara had learned from her. Daniel had seen her work often because she sourced some miniature pieces from his shop. Ellie helped occasionally, but only with painting or packaging.

Beyond that, almost no one.

Mara set the lantern down and gripped the edge of the table.

Whoever swapped this lantern knew exactly what they were doing.

They knew the glue Iris used.

They knew how to dismantle a miniature piece without destroying it.

They knew the hidden potential of the snowglobe bases.

Mara pressed her palms flat to the table, grounding herself.

She needed to talk to Daniel.

She had to.

Her instincts resisted the idea, but too many clues traced back to him. He had supplied the miniature lamp that Owen purchased. He had old snowglobes in his shop, some repaired over the years. He kept records of specialty items. He was one of the few people who understood the craft from the inside.

And Daniel had already admitted Owen asked him questions about repairs. About compartments. About tampering.

Mara picked up the lantern again and held it to the light.

The amber glue caught the sun, reflecting a faint golden hue across her fingertips.

"This was not random," she whispered.

Her fear sharpened into determination, clear and steady.

She placed the lantern gently into her coat pocket, locked up the bakery, and stepped out into the cold morning. Frostberry Hollow was just beginning to stir awake, but Mara felt as though she were walking into a secret world beneath the one everyone else saw.

The snow crunched under her boots as she made her way across the street to Daniel's shop. The antique lamps in the window cast a warm glow that contrasted with the icy air, inviting and yet somehow unsettling now that she understood more. She hesitated at the door, her breath fogging the glass.

Then she pushed inside.

Daniel was behind the counter polishing a clock face, his movements calm and methodical. He looked up at Mara with a warm expression that faltered when he saw the tension on her face.

"Mara," he said softly. "Are you all right?"

She stepped closer, her hand inside her pocket, fingers curled around the small lantern.

"I need to ask you something," she said.

Something in her voice made his brow tense slightly.

"Of course," he said. "What is wrong?"

Mara removed the lantern from her pocket and placed it on the counter between them.

Daniel stared at it.

The silence stretched.

He did not reach for it. He did not ask what it was. He simply stared at it with a stillness that made Mara's pulse race.

Finally, he exhaled.

"You found it," he said.

Mara's breath hitched. "You recognize it?"

Daniel nodded slowly.

"That is not your original lantern," he said. "Someone altered it."

"I know," Mara said.

Daniel glanced up at her, his expression conflicted.

"Mara," he said carefully, "where did you get this one?"

"It was inside Owen's snowglobe," she said. "In place of the lamp I made."

Daniel closed his eyes briefly. When he opened them, something guarded lingered behind the softness.

"So he did it," Daniel said with a quiet heaviness. "He really went through with it."

Mara felt her pulse quicken. "Went through with what?"

Daniel rubbed the back of his neck.

"Owen came to me about a week before the brunch," he said. "He brought me a snowglobe. Not yours. One someone else had made. He said he wanted it repaired, but the request felt strange. He asked me specifically how to remove a miniature safely and how to reattach it without leaving a trace."

Mara swallowed hard. "Did you help him?"

"I refused to do it for him," Daniel said. "I told him snowglobe repair was delicate work. That he should take it to you if it was your aunt's design. But he insisted he needed privacy. He asked what tools he would require. What glue to use. How long the binding would take to set."

Mara felt as if the air around her had grown too thin. "And you told him?"

Daniel grimaced. "I gave him general information. Nothing detailed. But I saw the look in his eyes. He was determined. And he had already purchased some of the materials from me."

Mara felt cold.

"So the glue used on this lantern," she said quietly, "he got it from you."

Daniel nodded, shame flickering across his face.

"I never imagined he would use it like this," Daniel said. "He told me he needed to fix something sentimental. He lied. I should have seen through it."

Mara stared at him, her heart pounding.

"Someone else knew how to do this too," she whispered. "Someone else searched my bakery. Someone else handled snowglobes."

Daniel looked at her with a steady, somber expression.

"Mara," he said gently, "whoever altered that lantern knew your aunt's techniques. They knew her glue. They knew how she worked."

Mara pressed a trembling hand to her chest.

"That means the killer does too," she whispered.

Daniel nodded.

"And that," he said softly, "is exactly what you should tell Connor."

Mara felt her breath slow, settle, and sharpen into something focused.

Whoever had done this was not an outsider. They were someone who understood Iris's craft deeply. Someone who had watched. Someone who had learned.

Someone who could walk into the bakery without looking suspicious.

A chill ran down her spine.

This mystery was not about land deeds alone.

It was about someone who knew how to hide secrets inside a snowglobe.

Someone very close to the town.

Possibly very close to Mara.

She stepped away from the counter.

"I need to think," she whispered.

Daniel nodded, concern lining his features.

"Do not walk around alone," he said. "If the person who did this thinks you know anything..."

Mara did not let him finish.

She stepped into the cold morning air, her breath forming a cloud in front of her.

The snowglobe had been tampered with by someone who knew exactly how to do it.

And Mara now understood something she had not dared think before.

The killer was not just someone connected to Owen.

The killer was someone connected to Iris.

* * *

Mara carried the tiny lantern back to the bakery with careful steps, as if the miniature piece could crumble in her palm if she dared rush. Snow muffled the world around her, settling thick on rooftops and drifting across the sidewalks with gentle persistence. The cold air pinched her cheeks and filled her lungs with a crisp sharpness that helped push back the fog of fear gathering behind her thoughts.

She wanted to think. She needed to think.

But each step sent her mind looping through the same burning questions.

Why had someone gone to such trouble to remove the lantern?

Why hide a clue inside her snowglobe?

Why use her aunt's work at all?

And most unsettling of all:

Who knew snowglobes well enough to pull off the alteration so cleanly?

The possibilities twisted through her thoughts in tight, overlapping circles. It was no longer just a matter of who disliked Owen or who stood to gain from land deeds. Someone had handled her globe. Someone had used her craft as if it belonged to them.

She reached the bakery and unlocked the door with a steadying breath. Inside, warmth wrapped around her like a blanket. The ovens hummed their familiar low tones. The scent of earlier baking still lingered, although it did little to soothe her rattled nerves.

Ellie was already inside waiting, perched on a stool with her coat folded across her lap. She looked up at once when Mara entered.

"There you are," Ellie said, relief loosening her shoulders. "I was starting to worry."

Mara slipped inside and shut the door gently behind her.

"I walked slowly," she said. "My head feels like it is carrying too much information at once."

Ellie studied her face, frowning softly. "Daniel did not upset you, did he?"

"No," Mara said. "He helped more than he realizes. But what he told me… it confirms something I did not want to believe."

Mara set the tiny lantern on the baking counter between them. Ellie leaned forward, studying it with a mix of awe and confusion.

"That is the piece?" Ellie asked softly. "The one that was removed from the globe?"

"Yes," Mara said. "Daniel helped me remove the adhesive residue on the base. It is glue. Not any normal craft glue. My aunt used it years ago when building her most detailed designs."

Ellie blinked. "So whoever removed the lantern... they had glue like that. Which means they had access to supplies she used."

Mara nodded.

"This glue was expensive," Mara said. "Hard to find. My aunt only ordered it from a specialized shop three towns over. She used it for the tiny pieces she wanted to keep permanent. She applied it in thin layers. She always complained about how long it took to dry even though it lasted decades once set."

Ellie traced one finger near the edge of the lantern, careful not to touch it. "And this glue is on the bottom of the lantern. Meaning whoever removed it replaced it at some point."

"Yes," Mara whispered. "And the glue is old. My aunt made that globe more than six years ago. That means someone altered it around the same time... or they removed the lantern more recently but the residue left behind belonged to the original adhesive."

Ellie went still.

"Mara," she said. "Your aunt gave away many of her globes. Some she sold. Some she donated. Some she gifted to friends and neighbors."

"I know," Mara said. "Which means someone in this town had access to her work. Someone who could have tampered with one of those pieces years ago. Maybe even before I moved here."

Ellie pressed her hand to her chest, startled. "You think this clue… this alteration… was made long before Owen collapsed?"

"I think it might have been prepared," Mara said. "Waiting for the right time or person. And Owen found it. Or took it. Or was given it."

Ellie let out a long breath.

"So who?" Ellie asked. "Who knew your aunt's techniques besides you? She must have talked with someone. She must have shared even a little about her snowglobes with people she trusted."

Mara turned away from the counter slowly and walked toward the shelves where old tools sat, many still in their original positions from when Iris had used them. Mara paused at the top shelf, fingers brushing along the wooden handles worn smooth by years of use.

"My aunt was private," Mara said. "She taught me much, but she never openly showed her deeper methods to many people. Some watched her out of curiosity. Some admired her pieces. But she never taught classes or shared her materials widely."

Ellie frowned. "But others could have seen her workbench. Or helped her pack boxes. Or assisted during a busy season."

"Yes," Mara said. "There were a few people. A few who visited her often."

She turned and began listing them quietly.

"The postmaster sometimes helped her deliver packages around the holidays. Harriet visited her for event donations. Mark bought custom pieces for his store window displays years ago. Daniel supplied her with several miniatures because he had old stock from estate sales."

Ellie's brows lifted.

"Wait," Ellie said softly. "Daniel."

Mara shook her head immediately.

"No," she said. "Do not misunderstand. Daniel helped me today. He told me the truth. He answered my questions. And he admitted Owen asked him about repairing globes."

"Yes," Ellie said. "But that means Daniel has knowledge. He knows how your aunt made them. He knows how the pieces work. He knows how to attach and remove components."

Mara felt a tightness form at the base of her throat.

"I know," she said quietly. "But Daniel is not the only one who could have learned."

Ellie approached her slowly.

"Did you ask him if he ever repaired globes for your aunt?" Ellie asked.

"Yes," Mara said. "He did. Twice. She brought him pieces she could not replace easily. Miniatures that had broken over the years. He repaired the bases, the hinges. He learned a few of her methods. Not all. But enough."

Ellie let that sink in.

"That does not mean he did this," Ellie said. "But it does mean he could have been one of a few who understood the inner structure."

Mara nodded slowly.

"I cannot start accusing everyone," she said. "At least not until I understand the clue fully. The paper mentioned land. It must connect to the mining title symbol."

Ellie's eyes widened. "The one we saw yesterday."

"Yes," Mara said. "The carved symbol. A circle with a vertical line and two small strokes. It matched the old mining claim."

"So the lantern... the clue... and the mining claim are all connected," Ellie whispered.

"Yes," Mara said. "Someone used the lantern compartment to hide land information. They wanted it kept secret."

Ellie pressed a hand to her forehead.

"But who would want an old mining claim?" Ellie asked. "What could it possibly matter today?"

Mara swallowed.

"Mineral rights," she said. "Water rights. Property lines. Maybe something deeper. Something buried."

Ellie's voice dropped.

"Tessa's well."

"Yes," Mara said. "And Harriet mentioned Owen pushing her to support development near Frostberry Creek. And Mark has been struggling with eviction papers connected to Owen's deals."

Ellie sank onto the stool, overwhelmed.

"Mara," Ellie said softly, "this goes beyond jealousy or business rivalry. There is something big here. Something Owen was chasing. And someone wanted him to stop."

Mara wrapped her arms around herself, trying to steady her heartbeat.

"I do not think Owen was the only target," she said quietly. "I think he was the most immediate."

Ellie stared at her, eyes wide.

"And you think whoever wanted that snowglobe thinks you know more than you do."

"Yes," Mara whispered. "I know because they broke into the bakery and searched my materials. They were looking for something. Another clue maybe. Or one of Iris's hidden designs."

Ellie's expression softened with worry.

"You cannot do this alone."

"I am not alone," Mara said. "I have you and Jenna. But I also have to keep pushing. Not because I want to... but because I am already involved whether I like it or not."

Ellie took a slow breath. "So what happens now?"

Mara picked up the tiny lantern again, studying the rough edges where it had been removed.

"I need to understand why my aunt's work was chosen," Mara said softly. "Whoever altered this globe knew the construction very well. It was not a random person."

Ellie nodded. "That narrows the list."

"Yes," Mara said. "And once we know who could have done it, everything else might fall into place."

Outside, snow pattered softly against the bakery windows. Inside, the ovens hummed with their usual warmth, but the air felt charged with something else.

A turning point.

A quiet shift.

A realization that the clues were no longer scattered threads but strands beginning to tighten toward a single truth.

Mara held the little lantern between her fingers and breathed in deeply.

"Someone in this town built the hiding place," she whispered. "And now I need to find out who."

Behind her, Ellie squared her shoulders.

"Then we will," Ellie said softly. "Together."

* * *

Mara left Daniel's shop with the small cloth wrapped lantern piece tucked safely inside her pocket. The air outside felt colder now, sharper somehow, as if the winter wind had overheard her conversation and wanted to push her back toward the truth she was beginning to fear.

The streetlights glowed softly through the falling snow, casting warm halos across the street. Frostberry Hollow always looked peaceful on nights like this, with its small shops and their softly lit windows. But tonight the shadows seemed longer. The gentle sounds of the town seemed distant. Everything felt too quiet.

She pulled her scarf tighter and walked briskly toward the bakery, boots crunching across the fresh layer of snow. The lantern piece felt heavier with each step, as if knowledge itself gained weight when carried.

When she reached the bakery door, she paused, her breath forming a thin fog in the air. For a moment she hesitated. The building stood dark except for one soft light left on in the display case. She unlocked the door and stepped inside, drawing a long breath of the familiar scent of sugar and spice.

Ellie and Jenna sat at the center table, leaning over photos and notebooks. They looked up immediately.

"There you are," Jenna said. "You look frozen. Come sit down."

Ellie pushed a steaming mug toward her. "Honey ginger tea. You need something warm."

Mara slipped into the chair, grateful for both the warmth and her friends.

"Tell us," Ellie said quietly. "What happened with Daniel?"

Mara set the lantern piece on the table between them.

Jenna leaned in. "That is the lantern? The actual piece from inside your snowglobe?"

"Yes," Mara said. "And the glue on its base is older than it should be. My aunt used that adhesive years ago. No one else uses it now, not unless they learned from her."

Ellie pressed a hand to her mouth. "That means someone who knows her work touched your snowglobe."

Mara nodded. "Someone who understands how the bases open. How to pry the piece out without destroying the structure. This was not random. It was careful. Skilled."

Jenna exhaled slowly. "So we narrow down who knows snowglobe construction. Iris, obviously. You, of course. Daniel knows the mechanics. But who else?"

Mara cupped her hands around the mug.

"A few people," she said. "Not many. My aunt taught a handful of workshops over the years. She helped a few locals repair old globes. And according to Daniel, she left some notes behind that Owen tried to get from him."

Ellie leaned back in her chair, thinking.

"When would Owen have had contact with your aunt?" she asked.

"I do not know," Mara said. "But the more I learn, the more it feels like he was digging into things far earlier than any of us realized."

Jenna tapped the table with her fingertips.

"And someone else has been digging too," she said quietly. "Someone who broke into your supply room. Someone who wanted to see if you had tools or pieces connected to the snowglobe."

Mara nodded. "They were searching for something. Maybe another clue. Maybe another miniature. Maybe even another globe."

Ellie turned toward her fully now.

"You think there are more clues hidden in the snowglobes?" Ellie asked.

Mara swallowed.

"I do not know," she said. "But I know this. Someone was willing to tamper with my snowglobe. Someone was willing to break into my bakery. And someone wanted whatever was inside Owen's briefcase. That takes planning. It takes intention. And it takes knowledge."

Jenna frowned. "Knowledge of miniature work."

"Yes," Mara said. "Someone who knows exactly how these are built."

Silence settled over them for a moment, heavy and cold like the snow thickening outside.

Ellie finally spoke.

"Mara," she said gently, "who knew your aunt well enough to learn all this?"

Mara let the question linger.

Faces flickered through her memory. People who admired Iris's work. People who visited the bakery when it still belonged to her aunt. People connected to land disputes. People connected to Owen.

Her aunt had lived quietly, but she had been well loved. Many had passed through her doors over the years.

But there were only a few who had ever studied her craft closely.

Mara's pulse quickened.

"I need to check something in the workshop," she said, standing abruptly.

Her friends rose with her, following as she moved toward the dim hallway and flicked on the light. The workshop looked as she had left it earlier, though the memory of the break in stained every corner.

She moved to her aunt's old cabinet, knelt down, and pulled out a thin wooden box with a carved lid. Inside were scraps from snowglobes her aunt had repaired or dismantled over the years. Broken miniatures. Old bases. And several lantern pieces in various stages of wear.

She selected one, held it up to the light, then placed it beside the one she had brought from Daniel's shop.

The resemblance was undeniable.

Same style. Same weight. Same old glue.

Ellie leaned closer. "It matches."

Jenna swallowed hard. "So whoever removed the miniature lantern from your snowglobe used the same adhesive Iris used long ago. That means they learned from her."

Mara nodded.

"And the break in proves they were looking for something related to her technique," she added.

Ellie looked suddenly uneasy. "Which means the person who tampered with the snowglobe could be someone who knew Iris very well."

"And someone who knew Owen," Jenna added. "Because they wanted the same clue he was carrying."

Mara felt a chill settle deep in her chest.

"It is someone here," she whispered. "Someone from Frostberry Hollow."

Ellie placed a comforting hand on her shoulder.

"We will figure out who," Ellie said softly. "But first you need to tell Connor what you discovered."

Mara took a shaky breath.

"No," she said. "Not yet."

Jenna blinked. "Not yet? Why not?"

"Because," Mara said quietly, "every time I give him information, the danger circles closer to me. We need to understand more before we hand this over."

Ellie and Jenna exchanged glances.

"What are you thinking?" Ellie asked.

Mara stepped back, holding the lantern piece in her palm.

"My aunt left patterns behind," she said. "She left old designs that she said were only experiments. But what if those patterns were more than decorative ideas? What if Iris created a system? A type of code? And what if someone else figured it out?"

Jenna's eyes widened.

"You mean the lantern itself was part of the code?" Jenna asked. "And the person who removed it knew how to read it?"

"Yes," Mara said. "And if they understood that, then they also know where to look for the next piece."

Ellie shivered.

"This is becoming frightening," Ellie whispered.

Mara closed her hand around the miniature lantern and met their eyes.

"The killer knows snowglobe construction very well," she said softly. "Too well. Better than anyone should."

Jenna sat down slowly, her breath uneven.

"Mara," she said, "if someone learned your aunt's craft with this much precision… we are not dealing with a stranger."

Mara nodded.

"We are dealing with someone who has been here all along."

The room went silent except for the soft ticking of the clock on the shelf.

Outside, the snow fell heavier, cloaking the town in quiet.

Inside, the truth finally began to take shape.

Someone from Frostberry Hollow understood the lantern code.

Someone who had once learned from Iris.

Someone who knew exactly how to hide secrets in plain sight.

Mara felt her heart pound harder at the realization.

She was not chasing shadows anymore.

She was chasing someone who knew her family's craft almost as well as she did.

And that person had killed to protect the secret.

Chapter 17

Frostberry Creek Woods waited at the edge of town like a secret the land had never fully surrendered. The tall pines rose in dark silhouettes against the pale winter sky, their branches heavy with fresh snow that drifted down in soft quiet pieces whenever a breeze stirred. The air carried a faint scent of sap and cold earth, a smell older than the town itself.

Mara stood at the treeline gripping her coat tighter as the early afternoon light dimmed behind thickening clouds. Jenna and Ellie had wanted to follow her, but after an hour of decoding the lantern symbol together, it became clear that the final step belonged to her alone. The clue revealed a simple set of directions from the creek to the roots of an old pine marked with a carved lantern shape. Only one tree in the woods had that carving. Her aunt had shown it to her years ago during a walk full of stories and winter laughter.

Now Mara approached it with a different kind of breath in her chest.

The woods were quiet. Almost too quiet. The world seemed to hold itself still as she stepped between trunks, crunching snow under her boots. A thin mist hovered low along the ground, weaving through the roots and fallen logs.

She followed the path along Frostberry Creek, a narrow winding thread of frozen water that glittered like a pane of glass. Her breath puffed out in small white clouds that vanished in the cold. She used her gloved hands to brush away pine branches, her heart pounding in quick, sharp rhythms.

She replayed the decoded clue in her mind.

Lantern's root where winter sleeps.

Turn the soil where the shadows meet.

Seek the box of stolen years.

Truth lies quiet beneath old fears.

She knew exactly where the lantern carving was. Her aunt had etched a tiny lantern into the bark decades ago, shaping it with the same steady hand she used for miniature pieces. Iris had always said the woods held stories for those who listened. Now Mara hoped those stories would include the truth.

She reached the familiar clearing after several minutes of careful hiking. There, at the center, stood the pine tree with the carved lantern. Time had worn the edges of the symbol, softening the lines, but the shape was clear.

A lantern. Just like the missing miniature.

Snow covered the ground around the tree, undisturbed and

smooth. Mara crouched down and brushed away the top layer, revealing the dark soil beneath. Her fingers trembled.

"Old fears," she murmured, repeating the final line of the clue. "Old fears are buried here."

She dug through the soft snow with slow, deliberate motions. Her gloves grew damp, and the frost bit at her fingers even through the fabric. She pushed aside roots and clumps of frozen soil until something solid tapped against her fingertips.

Mara froze.

She withdrew her hand and reached back in.

A metal edge.

Her breath caught.

Heart pounding, she cleared away more dirt and uncovered the corner of a small box made of aged metal, speckled with rust. She dug around it carefully until she could lift it from the earth.

It felt cold and heavy. Heavier than its size should allow.

She brushed off the remaining dirt and snow from the lid. No lock. Just a simple clasp.

"Please... please have answers," she whispered.

She opened it.

Inside lay a stack of folded papers, bound with a string. She lifted the bundle gently and unfolded the first sheet.

Her throat tightened.

These were land deeds.

Old ones. Some handwritten. Some stamped with official seals. Others marked with names she recognized from Frostberry Hollow's earliest families.

And several were clearly forged.

Signatures did not match. Dates overlapped improperly. Transfer approvals were missing. Legal language appeared copied and pasted from mismatched sources. And at the bottom corner of many documents was the same mark she had seen in the snowglobe clue. A lantern symbol. A code.

Owen Barrow had been tied to fraudulent land transfers.

Tessa's land.

Mark's building.

Several creekside properties.

Even festival grounds mentioned quietly by Harriet.

He had been buying and selling land with forged deeds. And someone else had been in on it.

Mara sifted deeper into the box.

A thin envelope rested at the bottom. She opened it with trembling fingers.

Inside were copies of financial ledgers, transaction slips and handwritten notes. Some identified Owen's name. Others referred to additional partners by only their initials.

She scanned for Harriet's initial. For Tessa's. For Mark's.

But she found another letter instead.

A single S.

Mara's breath hitched.

S for Snowglobe?

S for Sheriff?

S for Samwell, the lawyer from the next town?

S for someone she did not know?

The woods creaked softly as wind rustled the branches overhead.

Mara crouched lower over the box, shielding it with her body against the cold. She turned the last paper.

It showed a map of Frostberry Creek Woods with a red X over the clearing where she now knelt. Someone had planned to retrieve this box. Someone had known it existed.

Her aunt must have hidden it for a reason. Perhaps Iris had learned the truth and wanted to keep it safe until someone trustworthy found it.

Mara felt a swell of grief and determination rise together.

"Iris knew," she whispered. "She knew something terrible."

A branch cracked behind her.

Mara stiffened.

Slowly, she lowered the papers and stood.

The clearing shifted. The air felt heavier. She sensed movement rather than heard it.

When she turned, someone stepped between the trees, blocking the path she had taken into the woods.

The shape of the figure grew clearer as they approached. A heavy coat. Dark boots. Snow clinging to the edges of their sleeves.

Mara's pulse crashed into her ears.

"You should not have come here," the figure said quietly.

She recognized the voice.

Everything inside her tightened.

"You," she whispered. "It was you all along."

The figure stepped closer, cutting off her escape, their breath curling into the cold air like smoke.

Mara backed toward the carved pine tree, clutching the metal box to her chest.

"What did you do to Owen?" she asked, her voice trembling but steady enough to reach the clearing's edges.

The figure shook their head slowly, eyes glinting under the winter light.

"What I had to do," they said. "And you should have stayed out of this."

Mara tightened her grip on the box, her breath quick and cold.

The killer stepped fully into the clearing, blocking her only exit path.

Snow drifted down around them, quiet as breath.

The woods listened.

And Mara realized she was standing face to face with the person who had destroyed Owen, stolen her snowglobe, and broken into her bakery.

The truth had brought her here.

But the truth was not finished with her yet.

Chapter 18

The cold pressed in from every side. Frostberry Creek Woods held its breath around Mara, the tall trees rising like dark watchtowers beneath the silver glow of the winter moon. The brittle snow cracked faintly under her boots as she backed away from the figure blocking her only exit.

The killer stepped forward, gloved hands still but tense, their breath forming steady clouds in the night air. The metal box with the forged deeds lay open at Mara's feet, its papers exposed to the cold.

"So," the figure said, voice low but strangely calm, "you found it. I suppose I should not be surprised. Your aunt always said you had a stubborn streak."

The sound of that voice sent a hard chill through Mara's ribs. Recognizable. Familiar. A voice she had heard at community meetings, at festival planning, at the charity brunch. A voice that had once spoken kindly to her on her first week in Frostberry Hollow.

She could barely breathe.

"You," Mara whispered. "It was you all along."

They removed a glove slowly, revealing a trembling hand.

"Do not look at me like that," they said sharply. "You have no idea how many lives Owen ruined. How many futures he crushed. You think you know this town, but you have only touched the surface."

Mara steadied her breath, though fear pushed hard against her ribcage.

"Tell me," she said softly. "Tell me the truth."

The killer blinked, surprised by her calm tone. The wind rustled dry branches overhead, shifting snow through the air like scattered dust.

"All right," they said. "You want the truth. You came all this way for it."

They took a half step closer.

"Owen Barrow stole land from families who trusted him," they continued. "Promised them profit and returned nothing. He forced businesses under so he could buy properties cheap. He manipulated town officials. He was planning to use the deeds in that box to take ownership of the entire stretch of land around the creek."

Mara frowned. "You mean Frostberry Creek Woods."

"Yes," they said, voice tightening. "The last undeveloped section. My family's section. Our land was supposed to be passed down. It was meant to stay untouched. And Owen stole it. He threatened to bury us in legal fees until we caved."

They let out a bitter laugh.

"It was my father's land," they said. "He trusted Owen. Signed papers he thought were routine. Owen switched them. And by the time anyone realized, it was too late."

The pieces began falling together in Mara's mind.

"This was revenge," she whispered. "This entire thing."

"Revenge," the killer said softly, "and survival."

They moved one step closer, hands trembling.

"I tried to stop him peacefully," they said. "I argued. I begged. He did not care. He wanted the woods. He wanted the creek. He wanted everything. He even visited Daniel, asking about tools to break into snowglobes, because he knew someone else had hidden evidence against him. I did not know who at first. But then I saw your globe at the auction."

Mara swallowed. "So you took it."

"Of course I did," they said. "When Owen walked away from the table, I saw my chance. But he must have suspected. He must have realized the globe held something. That is why he opened it first."

Mara's gaze dropped to the metal box. The forged deeds. The fraudulent signatures. The proof that tied Owen to illegal land theft.

"And then you killed him," Mara whispered.

Silence fell thick and heavy.

The killer's jaw tightened.

"I did what I had to do," they said. "You cannot understand what he cost us. What losing that land did to my family. My father never recovered from the betrayal. He died thinking he had failed us. And Owen walked around town like nothing had happened."

Mara shook her head, voice quiet.

"But poisoning him," she said. "Breaking into my bakery. Putting me through this. You became what he was."

A flash of anger passed through their eyes.

"I am nothing like him."

"Then prove it," Mara said. "Walk away from this with me. There is still time to make the right choice."

They stared at her, stunned by the softness in her voice.

For a moment, Mara thought she might have reached them.

But then their shoulders squared.

"You are too late," they said. "I cannot let you leave with that box. You know too much."

They stepped forward.

Mara stumbled back, her boots slipping on the frozen ground. Fear gripped her chest, sharp and cold. She glanced around, calculating. No exit. No clear path through the dense trees. The night felt tighter. Darker.

"You do not need to do this," Mara said, keeping her voice

steady. "Please. You have suffered enough. Let the truth come out the right way."

"The right way?" The killer laughed bitterly. "The police protect people like Owen. The powerful. The ones with money. The ones who manipulate records. I tried everything. He left me no choice."

They were only a few steps from her now.

Mara forced herself to breathe.

"Look at me," she said gently. "I am not your enemy. I want the truth out too. For everyone he hurt."

The killer hesitated.

A single breath.

A single moment where everything hung in balance.

Then a twig snapped behind them.

Both heads jerked toward the sound.

A flashlight beam cut through the trees.

"Mara," a strong voice called, rough with urgency. "Stay where you are."

Connor.

Relief flooded Mara's body so fast her knees nearly buckled.

The killer spun toward the light, startled.

"How did he find us?" they whispered.

"My phone," Mara breathed. "I never turned off location."

The killer cursed under their breath.

Connor stepped into view, hands up in a calming gesture, but tension sharp in his eyes.

"Put your hands where I can see them," Connor said. "Do not move."

The killer backed away from Mara, breath fast and uneven.

"No," they said. "You cannot take me in. Not after everything he did."

Connor stepped forward carefully.

"I know what Owen did," Connor said quietly. "I know now. And I know you lost things you can never recover. But this is not the way to make it right."

The killer's chest heaved.

Mara stood still, afraid even a shift in weight would escalate the moment.

"You have no idea what I have lost," the killer whispered.

"Then tell me," Connor said. "But put the weapon down first."

Mara's heart clenched. She had not even noticed the killer reaching for something beneath their coat. A small tool. A blade used for opening locked boxes. Not large. Not designed for violence. But desperate hands could turn anything dangerous.

Connor kept his hands steady.

"We can fix this," he said. "Not perfectly. Not painlessly. But legally. Safely."

The killer shook their head, breath trembling.

"You cannot fix land that is gone," they said. "You cannot fix a stolen legacy."

"No," Connor said gently. "But you can stop this from becoming worse."

There was a long, fragile pause.

Wind rustled the branches overhead.

Mara pressed her hands together, praying silently.

Then, slowly, the killer's fingers loosened around the tool. It dropped into the snow with a soft, muffled thud.

Connor exhaled in relief.

"Thank you," he said softly.

He moved forward, placing one hand behind the killer's back and guiding them toward the treeline. The killer did not resist. Their shoulders sagged under the weight of years of anger, pain and betrayal.

Mara watched in silence, shaking with a blend of fear, exhaustion and empathy she could not fully name.

Connor settled the killer beside a fallen tree and read their rights softly. The trees around them stood tall and still, the woods witnessing a conclusion that had been building long before Mara ever arrived in Frostberry Hollow.

Once the cuffs were secured, Connor turned to Mara.

"Are you hurt?" he asked.

She shook her head, though her voice was faint.

"No," she whispered. "Just shaken."

Connor approached her gently, helping her sit on a cold fallen log.

"You should not have come here alone," he said.

"I had to," she said. "The clues led me here."

Connor let out a slow breath.

"You are lucky," he said quietly. "This could have ended very differently."

Mara looked toward the metal box lying half buried in the snow. The deeds. The proof. The tangled threads of Frostberry Hollow's hidden history.

"I did not want to be part of any of this," she whispered. "But I could not ignore it."

Connor nodded.

"That is why you found the truth," he said. "Because you care."

Mara rubbed her cold hands together, finally letting her breath steady.

"Is it really over?" she asked.

"Yes," Connor said. "It is over now."

Behind them, the killer sat in silence, their breath rising in faint white clouds.

Mara looked out into the woods. Snow fell gently around them, softening the sharp edges of the night.

For the first time in days, she felt something inside her loosen.

The fear began to ebb.

And in its place grew a quiet, fragile relief.

She had survived the truth.

The bakery would survive.

Her aunt's legacy would endure.

And as Connor led her back toward the path, Mara knew that whatever came next, Frostberry Hollow would never look the same.

But neither would she.

Chapter 19

The first morning after the arrest felt different in Frostberry Hollow. The snow fell in lighter flakes, drifting peacefully past the old lampposts and rooftops. The world seemed gentler, as if the storm that had raged through the town had finally exhausted itself and left behind a soft, cautious calm.

Mara arrived at the bakery just as dawn began to brighten the sky. Her boots crunched in the settled snow, and her breath curled in the cold air in faint, silvery ribbons. She paused at the door, gloved hand resting on the familiar handle, letting herself breathe in the quiet.

She had been awake most of the night replaying the events in the woods. The confrontation. The fear that had cut through her in cold waves. The shock of Connor appearing in time. The relief that had hollowed her out afterward. Her heart still felt tender, bruised from the suddenness of it all.

But when she opened the bakery door and stepped inside, the warmth lifted her spirits at once.

The Cozy Nook smelled of cinnamon and brown sugar. Mara had prepared dough the night before and set it to rise in the refrigerator, knowing that reopening the bakery would feel right. The ovens were already warming. The counters gleamed. The trays waited.

The bakery looked like home.

Mara exhaled slowly, feeling something inside her loosen.

She rolled up her sleeves and started shaping the dough, focusing on each familiar motion. Folding. Pressing. Brushing each pastry with melted butter. It grounded her, drawing her away from the woods, away from the danger, and back into the life she had fought so fiercely to protect.

By the time the bell above the door chimed for the first time, the sun had stretched soft light across the floorboards and the scent of fresh pastries filled the air.

A bundle of winter clothes stepped inside. Then another. Then a third.

Mara blinked.

People were lining up.

A group of regulars stood near the door, stamping snow off their boots. A couple she had never seen before whispered happily to one another. A local teacher waved at her from the counter. A visiting family with ski gear in hand stepped into line, drawn by the smell alone.

"Mara," Mrs. Pennington said warmly from the front, "we came early. We knew it would be busy today."

"You knew?" Mara asked, surprised.

"We all talked," Mr. Pennington said. "People realized how much this bakery means to the town. We wanted to show our support."

Another woman chimed in. "You have been through so much, dear. We thought you might need to see your community."

A tall man nodded as he stepped forward. "You stayed strong. We want you to know the town noticed."

A rush of warmth filled Mara's chest. For days she had feared losing the bakery. Feared the whispers. Feared the suspicion. Feared being alone in the middle of something she had not asked for.

But now the bakery buzzed with life. With support. With warmth.

She wiped her hands on her apron and smiled at the crowd.

"Come in," she said softly. "Thank you for being here."

The morning passed in a gentle rush. She served scones and cinnamon rolls, poured coffee, and listened to people talk. Not in hushed whispers, but in bright, relieved voices.

"So glad they caught the real culprit," someone said.

"Unbelievable that they used those forged deeds," another murmured.

"I always said the bakery had nothing to do with it," a third insisted while tapping a mittened hand on the counter.

Tourists asked about the snowglobe auction. Locals asked if Mara planned to make another winter themed piece next year.

Children pressed their noses to the display case begging for cranberry scone cake slices.

By midday, Mara found herself laughing again.

Feeling again.

Belonging again.

Ellie arrived next, pushing her way through the crowd with a bag of craft supplies tucked under one arm.

"Look at this place," Ellie said, wide eyed. "This is better than the summer rush."

"You helped this happen," Mara said. "Both of you did."

Ellie waved off the praise with watery eyes. "Not true. You built this bakery. You kept going when things looked terrible. That is what people came here to support."

Jenna appeared right behind her wearing her usual scarf and holding a thermos.

"I brought tea," Jenna said. "And also myself, which is arguably more useful."

"Barely," Ellie teased.

Jenna gave her a dramatic glare. "I take that personally."

Mara laughed and pulled both women close in a warm, grateful hug.

"You two saved me," she whispered. "If you had not believed me... if you had not pushed me when I wanted to hide..."

"You did the brave part," Jenna said.

"We just brought snacks," Ellie added.

They worked the rest of the afternoon beside Mara, helping with customers and packaging orders. Jenna took new photos of the bakery with actual smiles behind the counter. Ellie made small decorative signs that read, Support Frostberry Hollow and Thank you for believing in us.

Everything felt lighter.

Everything felt possible.

Near closing, the crowd began to thin. The sun dipped low, casting ribbons of orange and gold across the snowy street. The bakery lamps glowed warmly, reflecting off the glass and filling the room with soft amber tones.

Mara wiped down the counter, exhaustion settling into her bones, but it was the pleasant sort of exhaustion. The kind she associated with accomplishment and comfort.

The bell chimed once more.

She looked up.

Connor Hale stepped inside.

His uniform jacket was dusted with snow, but he removed his hat as he entered, the gesture gentle, almost shy.

"Busy day," Connor said.

"Surprisingly busy," Mara replied with a small smile.

"You deserve it," he said.

Jenna elbowed Ellie lightly. "We should step into the kitchen," she whispered loudly.

"We should," Ellie agreed with obvious delight. "Very necessary kitchen tasks."

They disappeared before Mara could protest.

Connor approached the counter and looked at the remaining pastries.

"Got anything left?" he asked.

"I saved a cinnamon roll for you," Mara said quietly. "Jenna told me once you are addicted to them."

Connor chuckled. "She is not wrong."

Mara handed him the warm pastry on a plate. Connor accepted it but did not move away. Instead, he leaned slightly against the counter.

"I wanted to check on you," he said. "After yesterday. After everything."

"I am all right," Mara said softly. "Or getting there."

"I am glad," Connor said. "When I got the alert from your phone signal and realized you were heading into the woods alone... I do not think I have ever driven so fast."

Mara looked down, cheeks warming. "Thank you for coming."

"Always," Connor said quietly.

She lifted her eyes to his. In the warm glow of the bakery lights, he looked both strong and gentle, a mix she had not quite allowed herself to notice until this moment.

Connor took a small bite of the cinnamon roll. "Still the best pastries in town."

"Good," Mara said softly. "I need the bakery to thrive again."

"It will," he said. "People love this place. And they trust you."

"Do you?" she asked before she could stop herself.

Connor set the plate down.

He met her gaze fully.

"Yes," he said. "More than you know."

The warmth in his voice made something flutter in her chest.

Ellie and Jenna peeked from the kitchen doorway, pretending to rearrange napkins but watching with the subtlety of children spying on grown ups.

Mara sighed and laughed at the same time.

Connor glanced behind him and smiled. "Your friends care about you."

"I would be lost without them," Mara said.

"And now the town knows what you are capable of," Connor added. "You solved more of this case than anyone else. I cannot take credit for that."

"You kept me safe," Mara said quietly.

"That was never a question," Connor replied.

The moment stretched between them, warm and calm. The first calm Mara had felt in a long time.

Finally she asked, "Would you like coffee to go with that cinnamon roll?"

"I would," he said. "As long as it means I get to stay a little longer."

Mara poured him a cup.

The bakery, with its soft lights and gentle scents and warm wood, felt like the safest place in the world.

And for the first time since arriving in Frostberry Hollow, Mara felt the truth settle quietly in her chest.

This was her home.

Not just the bakery.

Not just the town.

The people.

The life she had begun to build among them.

The friendships.

The slow, steady spark of something new with a man who cared more than he showed.

She looked around and smiled.

Tomorrow would bring more baking, more laughter, and more healing.

But tonight, the bakery doors were still open, and the warmth inside glowed brighter than the snow outside.

She belonged here.

And the town, in its own quiet way, belonged to her too.

Chapter 20

Snow drifted past the bakery window in quiet spirals, soft enough to look dreamlike. The Cozy Nook Bakery had already closed for the evening, the last traces of cinnamon and warm sugar floating through the still air. Light from the upstairs workroom spilled down the stairwell, golden and inviting.

Mara climbed the steps slowly, holding a small box of materials against her chest. Her heart felt steady for the first time in weeks. The town was healing. The truth was known. The fear had loosened its grip. All that remained tonight was a sense of quiet renewal.

She reached the worktable and set her materials down. The room greeted her like an old friend. Brushes neatly cleaned. Miniatures lined up in small jars. A few stray flakes of snowdust still shimmered on the wooden surface.

At the center of the table sat a glass sphere she had prepared earlier. Empty. Waiting.

Mara placed her hands on the edges of the table and breathed deeply, letting the peace of the moment wash over her.

"This one is for me," she whispered.

For courage.

For healing.

For hope.

She began by arranging a small base of dark green felt, trimmed neatly around the curve. Then she chose the miniature she had kept tucked away for months, a tiny pine tree with branches dusted in soft white paint. She pressed it gently into place.

Next came a narrow wooden path, carved from a scrap piece her aunt Iris had once intended to use in a long forgotten design. Mara smiled as she aligned it beneath the tree.

"Thank you, Aunt Iris," she murmured. "You still guide me."

Her final touch was a small lantern, not identical to the stolen one, but similar enough that it made her chest ache in a good way. This lantern did not symbolize secrets. It symbolized what came after truth.

She glued the piece in carefully. Slow. Steady. Certain.

When she finally held the finished snowglobe in her hands, the tiny pine tree, lantern, and winding path shimmered beneath the soft swirl of snowflake glitter. It looked peaceful. But more than that, it looked brave.

A memory of the woods flashed behind her eyes. The cold bark of the pine roots. The fear when the killer stepped into the clearing. Connor's voice calling her name. The sound of handcuffs clicking at last.

She had survived all of it.

She turned the snowglobe slightly in her hands and smiled.

This winter no longer belonged to fear.

It belonged to her.

* * *

Footsteps sounded on the stairs.

Mara looked up as Ellie appeared at the top step, cheeks pink from the cold evening air and a small wrapped parcel in her gloved hands.

"You are still up here," Ellie said, her smile warm. "I thought I would find you working late."

"I was finishing something," Mara said. "Come look."

Ellie stepped closer and admired the snowglobe with wide, sincere delight.

"Mara," Ellie breathed, "it is beautiful. It feels like... everything you just lived through, turned into something gentle."

"That is what I hoped," Mara said softly.

Ellie placed her parcel on the table.

"I brought you something," she said. "I was not sure when to give it to you, but now seems right."

Mara unwrapped it carefully.

Inside was a miniature winter bench, carved in exquisite detail. The seat had faint wood grain, and the legs held a delicate silver frost effect.

"It reminded me of you," Ellie said. "Something steady to sit on while the world settles itself."

Mara touched the tiny bench with reverence.

"It is perfect," she said. "Thank you."

"And," Ellie added with a small grin, "I know you started that winter themed series of snowglobes. Consider this the first piece of inspiration for whatever comes next."

Mara felt her heart swell.

"You always know exactly what to bring," she said.

"Only because I pay attention," Ellie replied.

Mara placed the miniature on her shelf of future pieces. It glowed softly in the lamplight.

"Maybe tomorrow I will start another design," Mara said.

"I hope you do," Ellie replied. "You deserve a project that is only joyful."

A soft knocking came from the open stairwell.

"Are the two of you hiding from me again?" Jenna called as she climbed the steps, one gloved hand gripping the railing, her curls escaping her hat as usual.

"We are not hiding," Ellie said. "We are admiring Mara's newest masterpiece."

Jenna reached the table and gasped.

"Oh my goodness," she said. "You need to put that in a museum. Or sell it to a rich tourist. Or keep it forever. Actually keep it forever. It has main character energy."

Mara laughed. "It is just a snowglobe."

"No," Jenna said dramatically. "It is the snowglobe of a woman who solved a murder in the middle of winter and lived to bake again."

Mara shook her head, smiling. "I did not solve anything alone."

"You might as well have," Jenna said proudly. "Between your instincts, your snowglobe knowledge, your ability to run in the woods even though you claim to trip over flat floors... I stand by it. Detective skills."

"I do not need detective skills," Mara said lightly. "I just need peace."

Jenna put a hand over her heart. "You can have both. Peace and well honed investigative talents."

Ellie laughed, full of warmth. Mara joined in, the sound lightening something inside her chest.

As the laughter faded, Jenna picked up the finished snowglobe and turned it gently in her hands.

"You know," Jenna said softly, "this really does look like a beginning."

Mara felt her eyes sting.

"I think it is," she whispered.

* * *

Later that evening, after Ellie and Jenna left with promises to return in the morning, Mara carried the new snowglobe downstairs. She placed it in the cabinet near the register, where the morning sun would shine on it.

She turned off the lights one by one, letting the bakery fall into its warm twilight glow.

The ovens clicked softly.

The windows reflected the winter night.

The scent of vanilla and spice lingered in the calm air.

Mara walked to the front door and paused with her hand on the lock.

This place was hers.

Not just a bakery.

Not just a project inherited from her aunt.

It was a home. A refuge. A spark in the snowy world outside.

And she had fought to keep it.

She turned the lock, feeling steady and sure.

As she stepped outside, the town wrapped around her in soft, snowy silence. Lamp posts glowed gently through the falling flakes. The street looked peaceful. Safe.

A hint of excitement curled through her chest. Not fear. Not leftover tension.

Something different. Something like promise.

She glanced back at the bakery window. The faint shape of her snowglobe glimmered inside, blurred slightly by the frosty glass.

"Whatever comes next," she whispered to the snowy night, "I am ready."

And she truly was.

Winter in Frostberry Hollow no longer felt full of secrets waiting to pounce.

It felt like the start of something new. Something brave.

Something hers.

And in the warm glow spreading across her heart, Mara knew there would always be more stories in this town. More mysteries tucked between snow covered roots, old buildings and hidden histories.

But tonight, she closed her eyes, breathed in the winter air, and let herself rest.

Because tomorrow, she would wake to a new chapter.

And someday soon, she would be ready for another adventure.

Chapter 21

Seasonal Treats from the Bakery

A collection of treats
inspired by the moments that
shaped her winter mystery.

Winter has always brought out the best
in the Cozy Nook Bakery. The colder the
wind outside, the more the ovens glow,
filling the rooms with warmth, sweet
scents, and that quiet feeling of comfort
that seems to settle into your bones one
bite at a time. After everything that
happened this season, I learned
something important. Baking is more than a craft. It is
memory and courage and hope mixed together.

Many of you asked for the recipes behind the treats
mentioned throughout these pages. Some were created on
calm mornings. Others were born in the middle of chaos,
when a spoonful of sugar and a warm oven were the only
things that helped me steady my heartbeat. A few were my
aunt Iris's traditions, which she passed down to me with
gentle patience and a sparkle in her eye. I treasure them now
more than ever.

These recipes are more than ingredients and steps. They are pieces of moments that shaped this winter. The first brave morning after the charity brunch. The night I worked late by the glow of the snowglobe lamp. The afternoons spent with Ellie and Jenna, where laughter softened even the hardest questions. Every flavor holds a memory.

So take your time. Settle in. Warm your kitchen. Bake something that fills the air with comfort. And know that wherever you are, you have a place here at the Cozy Nook Bakery.

Welcome in.

* * *

Blackberry Winter Scones

Makes: 8 large scones

Inspired by: Chapter 3, Mara's early morning baking and the charity brunch

Ingredients

- 2 cups all purpose flour

- 1 tablespoon baking powder

- ¼ cup granulated sugar

- ½ teaspoon salt

- 6 tablespoons cold unsalted butter, cubed

- 1 cup fresh or frozen blackberries

- ¾ cup heavy cream

- 1 teaspoon vanilla extract

- 1 teaspoon lemon zest

- Extra cream and coarse sugar for brushing

Instructions

1 Heat oven to 400°F. Line a baking sheet with parchment.

2 In a large bowl whisk the flour, baking powder, sugar and salt.

3 Cut in the butter using a pastry cutter or fingertips until the mixture looks like coarse crumbs.

4 Gently fold in blackberries.

5 In a small bowl mix the cream, vanilla and lemon zest. Pour into the dry mixture.

6 Stir until the dough just comes together. Do not overmix.

7 Turn onto a floured board and shape into a 7 inch disk. Cut into 8 wedges.

8 Brush tops with cream and sprinkle with coarse sugar.

9 Bake 17 to 20 minutes, until golden around the edges.

10 Cool slightly before serving. Best eaten warm.

Cinnamon Swirl Rolls With Vanilla Glaze

Makes: 12 rolls

Inspired by: Chapter 3 and the charity brunch buffet

Dough Ingredients

• 3 cups all purpose flour

• ¼ cup granulated sugar

• 2¼ teaspoons instant yeast

• 1 teaspoon salt

• 1 cup warm milk

• ¼ cup melted butter

• 1 large egg

Filling Ingredients

• ½ cup softened butter

• ¾ cup brown sugar

• 1 tablespoon cinnamon

Glaze

• 1 cup powdered sugar

• 2 tablespoons milk

• ½ teaspoon vanilla extract

Instructions

1 In a large bowl whisk flour, sugar, yeast and salt.

2 Add warm milk, melted butter and egg. Mix until a soft dough forms.

3 Knead on a floured surface about 5 minutes until smooth.

4 Place in an oiled bowl, cover and rise 1 hour.

5 Roll the dough into a 10 by 14 inch rectangle.

6 Spread with softened butter, sprinkle with brown sugar and cinnamon.

7 Roll tightly from the long edge and slice into 12 rolls.

8 Arrange in a greased baking dish. Rise 30 minutes.

9 Bake at 375°F for 20 to 25 minutes.

10 Whisk glaze ingredients and drizzle over warm rolls.

Frostberry Hollow Snowflake Cookies

Makes: about 30 cookies

Inspired by: Decorations in Chapter 3 and the town's winter charm

Ingredients

- 2½ cups all purpose flour
- ½ teaspoon baking powder
- ¼ teaspoon salt
- ¾ cup unsalted butter, softened
- ¾ cup granulated sugar
- 1 large egg
- 1 teaspoon vanilla extract
- Optional: ½ teaspoon almond extract

Icing

- 1½ cups powdered sugar
- 1 to 2 tablespoons milk
- Few drops vanilla
- Blue or white decorative sugar

Instructions

1 Whisk flour, baking powder and salt.

2 Cream butter and sugar until light and fluffy.

3 Add egg and vanilla.

4 Add dry ingredients slowly.

5 Chill dough at least 1 hour.

6 Roll to ¼ inch thick and cut into snowflake shapes.

7 Bake at 350°F for 8 to 10 minutes.

8 Cool fully before icing.

9 Mix icing to a thick but pipeable consistency and decorate with simple lines or dot patterns.

Cozy Nook Hot Chocolate Mix

Makes: 6 to 8 servings

Inspired by: The comforting drinks Mara, Ellie and Jenna often share during stressful moments

Ingredients

- 1 cup powdered milk

- ½ cup powdered sugar

- ½ cup unsweetened cocoa powder

- ½ cup white chocolate chips

- ¼ teaspoon cinnamon

Instructions

1 Combine all dry ingredients in a bowl.

2 Store in an airtight jar.

3 To serve, mix 3 tablespoons of the blend with 1 cup hot milk.

New Beginnings Lemon Maple Muffins

Makes: 12 muffins

Inspired by: The "New Beginnings" snowglobe symbolism

Ingredients

- 2 cups all purpose flour

- 1 tablespoon baking powder

- ½ teaspoon salt

- ⅓ cup sugar

- 1 cup milk

- ¼ cup pure maple syrup

- ¼ cup melted butter

- 2 tablespoons lemon juice

- 1 tablespoon lemon zest

- 1 egg

Instructions

1 Heat oven to 375°F. Line a muffin tin.

2 Whisk the dry ingredients in one bowl.

3 Mix the milk, maple syrup, butter, lemon juice, zest and egg in another.

4 Combine wet and dry ingredients until just blended.

5 Spoon into cups and bake 16 to 20 minutes.

6 Cool and drizzle with a light lemon maple glaze if desired.

Maple Walnut Mini Tarts

Makes: 12 mini tarts

Inspired by: Mara's cozy winter flavor combinations

Ingredients

Crust:

- 1½ cups flour

- ¼ cup sugar

- ½ cup cold butter, cubed

- 1 egg yolk

- 2 to 3 tablespoons cold water

Filling:

- ½ cup chopped walnuts

- ⅓ cup maple syrup

- 2 tablespoons brown sugar

- 1 egg

- 1 teaspoon vanilla

Instructions

1 Heat oven to 350°F.

2 Blend flour, sugar and butter until crumbly.

3 Add egg yolk and water until dough forms.

4 Press dough into a mini muffin pan.

5 Mix walnuts, maple syrup, brown sugar, egg and vanilla.

6 Spoon filling into crusts.

7 Bake 15 to 18 minutes until golden.

Winter Spice Loaf

Makes: 1 loaf

Inspired by: Aunt Iris and the comforting flavors she passed down to Mara

Ingredients

- 1¾ cups flour

- 1 teaspoon baking soda

- ½ teaspoon baking powder

- ½ teaspoon salt

- 1 teaspoon cinnamon

- ½ teaspoon nutmeg

- ¼ teaspoon ground cloves

- ½ cup melted butter

- ½ cup brown sugar

- ¼ cup maple syrup

- 2 eggs

- ¾ cup buttermilk

- Optional: ½ cup chopped nuts or raisins

Instructions

1 Heat oven to 350°F. Grease a loaf pan.

2 Whisk flour, baking soda, baking powder, salt and spices.

3 In another bowl whisk melted butter, brown sugar, maple syrup and eggs.

4 Add dry ingredients alternating with buttermilk.

5 Stir gently. Fold in nuts or raisins if using.

6 Pour into the pan and bake 45 to 55 minutes.

7 Cool before slicing.

Chapter 22
Mara's Baking Tips for Winter Success

Winter in Frostberry Hollow brings early sunsets, deep stillness and cold air that can surprise even an experienced baker. Mara has learned that winter baking is its own special craft, filled with unique challenges and small joys. These are 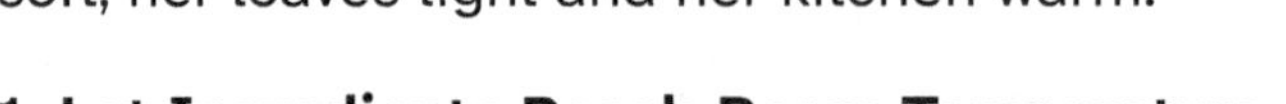 the techniques she uses each season to keep her pastries soft, her loaves light and her kitchen warm.

1. Let Ingredients Reach Room Temperature

In winter, butter and eggs take longer to warm up. Cold ingredients can make batter stiff or cause doughs to resist mixing. Mara sets everything out at least thirty minutes before baking so her pastries stay tender and her dough spreads evenly.

2. Use Warmed Mixing Bowls for Yeast Doughs

Yeast can be fussy when the air is cold. Mara rinses her mixing bowl with warm water before adding dough ingredients. This helps the yeast wake gently and rise properly, even when snow piles at the windows.

3. Avoid Overmixing Cold Batters

Cold temperatures often thicken batters faster. Overmixing leads to dense muffins or tough scones. Mara mixes only until the ingredients come together, keeping her pastries light and soft.

4. Check Oven Temperature Twice

Cold kitchens can make ovens run cooler when first preheating. Mara uses an oven thermometer in the winter months to make sure the inside reaches true baking temperature. This keeps her cinnamon rolls from underbaking and her shortbread from spreading.

5. Adjust Liquid Amounts on Dry Days

Winter air is noticeably drier. Flour absorbs more moisture, so Mara adds an extra teaspoon of milk or cream to doughs that feel stiff. It keeps her scones from crumbling and her loaves from drying out too quickly.

6. Warm Baking Sheets Before Shaping Cookies

Cold pans can cause butter to seize and cookies to spread unevenly. Mara warms baking sheets for a minute or two in the oven, then lines them with parchment before placing dough on top.

7. Let Flavors Rest Overnight When Possible

Winter spices bloom beautifully after resting. Mara often prepares spice loaf, ginger cookies or maple glaze the night before, letting the flavors deepen. The next day, everything tastes richer and more developed.

8. Protect Rising Dough from Drafts

A single cold draft can slow a rise dramatically. Mara places dough in her warmest corner, often near the gently humming dishwasher or beside a cooling oven, covered with a soft cloth to keep it from chilling.

9. Store Baked Goods Carefully

Winter air dries pastries quickly. Mara stores most of her goods in airtight containers while still slightly warm, trapping gentle moisture inside to keep everything tender.

10. Create a Cozy Atmosphere While You Bake

Mara believes winter baking is as much about warmth as it is about technique. She lights a soft candle, puts on gentle music and fills the bakery with the comfort of vanilla and spice. A calm baker always makes better pastries.

www.ingramcontent.com/pod-product-compliance
Lightning Source LLC
Chambersburg PA
CBHW071743190726
48292CB00003B/855